THE PERFECT VICTIM

DAVID SODERGREN

For George Taylor
Forever my best friend

1

———

BAXTER WATCHED THE GIRL EXIT THE SCHOOL GROUNDS, accompanied — as always — by that little curly-haired bitch. He scratched at the filth beneath his fingernails with a switchblade, inspecting the black muck he dug out.

"There she is," he muttered. "Like fucking clockwork."

He leaned back in the driver's seat of the nondescript white van — stolen, new plates — and tried to act casual as the teenagers filtered through the gates, laughing and screaming and chasing each other. A group of boys barreled past, one of them shoving the smallest kid into the side of the van. The impact resounded throughout the vehicle, and Baxter fought back the urge to get out and grab one of those fucking assholes by the throat.

But he couldn't be seen. Not after all the planning. This was it, the big day, months of research and preparation leading to this moment. They couldn't blow it, not now. And if they did, it sure as shit wasn't going to be *him* that fucked the whole operation up.

"Which one?" said Corvo, squinting through the grime-encrusted window at the parade of identically dressed young people bustling along the sidewalk. "They all look the same."

Baxter snorted in annoyance.

"Blonde ponytail, next to the redhead."

"I don't see her," said Corvo, his voice choked with phlegm. He wound down the window and spat, the glob of mucus landing on an unsuspecting girl's schoolbag. He turned to Baxter, grinning, most of his front teeth missing, the remaining few nothing but blackened stumps. "Hey, you see that? I got her right on the—"

Baxter smacked Corvo across his arm. It was a token gesture — the coiled, tense muscles beneath Corvo's thin sweater didn't register the blow — but Baxter knew violence was the only way to keep the bigger man in line. He had met plenty of assholes like Corvo through the years, but rarely as stupid, or as loyal. It was a dangerous combination, but, if harnessed correctly, one that could yield satisfactory results.

"She's right there," he said. "Want me to put on a neon sign and go slap her ass, you dumb motherfucker?"

"Fuck you," grumbled Corvo. "Don't need to hit me. I see her now."

Together they watched as the girl bounded down the street with the redhead, her ponytail bouncing with each step, skirt swishing above her knees. The hot summer sun beat down, turning the van interior into a clammy sweatbox.

"Do we follow?" asked Corvo, as if he had forgotten the plan already.

"Not yet."

"But she's getting away."

"We don't wanna act suspicious. We're just gonna sit here like two ugly bastards in a van until she takes the lane."

Corvo wiped sweat from his brow. It left a stain on his sleeve. "What if she doesn't?"

Baxter smiled. "She will."

He had watched the girl leave school every day for the last two months, always from a different vantage point, usually in a new disguise. Whereas some teenagers were unreliable, this one was a model of efficient predictability. She never cut class. Always went straight home.

She was the perfect victim.

He knew her whole routine. Out of school at three-forty Monday to Thursday, twelve-fifteen on a Friday. Today was Friday, the start of the weekend. The girl would head three blocks down Pendrew Street with her friend, and then the two would part at Schofield Lane, where she always took a shortcut through the industrial park. Where she went from there didn't matter. By that point, she would be bound and gagged and in the van, exactly as planned.

"What about now?" asked Corvo, drumming his fingernails nervously against the back of his phone.

"Just wait," said Baxter. His hand slipped, and the switchblade jabbed into his finger. He flinched, watching the blood ooze from the small wound before wiping it on his pant leg.

He allowed himself a smile.

"Just wait."

2

Katy Ketcher stopped in the middle of the sidewalk and fixed Jill with her most serious stare, the kind that said, *hey listen, this is important.*

"What's up?" said Jill, brushing a strand of wavy red hair from her eyes.

Katy frowned and looked at her feet. She kicked a stray pebble onto the road as a couple of boys raced past on their way home.

"It's nothing," she said, in a tone that suggested it *was* something.

Jill, being the good friend she was, played along. "Come on, you can tell me."

Katy considered taking her hand, but it was too hot to touch someone else. The temperature had to be nudging one-hundred, the sun a shimmering orange globe in the sky.

How long would it take for your eyes to melt if you looked straight at it?

It was a good question, and one she would return to later,

but right now there were more pressing matters. School was out for the weekend, but she wouldn't be able to relax and enjoy herself without getting something off her chest.

"I saw Jake talking with Leslie at lunch," she said with all the gravity the situation demanded.

Jill shrugged. "So?"

"*So*," said Katy, stretching the syllable out like bubblegum. "You think he's gonna ask her?"

"For what?" smiled Jill, adopting a guileless tone that always wound Katy up. "A sandwich? The secret to eternal life?"

Katy playfully shoved her friend and turned her back on her. "You're such a bitch. To the *dance*, obviously. You think they'll go together?"

"Hadn't really thought about it."

"I'm *serious*," said Katy. She knew Jill was only messing with her, but this was not the time. "She's so much prettier than me."

"That's true."

"What?"

Jill grinned and rolled her eyes theatrically. "I'm *kidding*. You're the prettiest princess in *all* the kingdom."

The sarcasm was not lost on Katy. "Shut up," she said. It was a lame retort, but the heat made it difficult to think of anything better.

She walked on, Jill scampering after her. Her friend's hand tugged on her schoolbag.

"Of course he's gonna ask you," said Jill. "You see the way he was staring at you in English?"

Katy stopped a moment, thoughtful. It was true. Jake could easily have kept turning to Leslie to ask for answers. She sat closer to him, after all. But no, he had pivoted further in his seat to ask *her*. That had to mean something, surely?

"I guess you're right," she said.

"I'm always right. That's why we're friends."

Katy tilted her head. "Do explain."

"You need *me* to stop *you* from making bad decisions."

"Uh-huh," said Katy. "And where were you that time I bleached my hair?"

Jill pulled a face. "I thought we agreed never to talk about... the incident."

"Yeah, well, I learned a valuable lesson. Never do anything you can pay to have someone else do for you."

"Words to live by. Hey, do you—"

But Katy had stopped again. She was dimly aware of Jill talking, but something had caught her interest. A van parked on the other side of the street. The once-white exterior was thick with dirt, and someone had written WASH ME in the filth with their finger. A man sat inside, his face obscured by the sun-streaked windows.

He's watching you.

The man turned away, suddenly interested in what was in the glove compartment. It was a dismal attempt to look inconspicuous.

Jill waved her hand in front of her friend's face. "Katy... Earth to Katy, you still with us?"

Katy glanced at her. "That van," she said quietly.

"Yes," agreed Jill. "That *is* a van. Would you like a round of applause?"

"The guy in it was staring at me."

"The windows are so dirty you can't even see in," said Jill. "You sure there's someone in there?"

"I saw movement."

"Probably some pervert with a schoolgirl fetish. Keira Page says all old men have one. It's Freudian, or something."

"Who's Keira Page?" said Katy, only half-listening, watching for motion from inside the van.

"You know, Ronnie Page's sister. Got fingered by Lenny Clark in the girls' locker room. She has a YouTube channel about gardening."

Katy finally looked away, giving Jill her most incredulous stare. "What?"

"It's true. She has thirteen subscribers to her YouTube channel. She's gonna take the gardening world by storm, or so she says."

"I wouldn't let Lenny Clark's fingers anywhere *near* me," Katy said absently. "He still picks his nose."

Jill leaned in close. "I heard he eats his boogers," she said.

Katy wasn't listening.

She could have *sworn* the man was watching her. Was there someone else beside him? She stepped off the sidewalk between two parked cars and stared at the van. The engine rumbled into life and the vehicle pulled out, nearly sideswiping a passing car in its haste to leave.

"Told you," said Jill. "It was just some old creep eating his lunch and touching himself."

"You're gross," said Katy. Jill took her by the arm, but Katy's eyes tracked the vehicle down the curiously silent street until it made a right turn and disappeared from view.

"He left when I noticed him."

Jill laughed. "Oh god, you're so paranoid. It's probably the paparazzi trying to get a shot of you. You'll be on the front page of TMZ by the time we get home. I can see the headline now — KETCHER DAUGHTER SEES VAN, OVERREACTS."

Katy smiled. "Sorry, I'm being dumb. You're right, as usual."

"And don't you forget it. What would you do without me?"

"I'd be rich and famous."

"You *are* rich and famous."

Katy took Jill by the shoulders and yelled in mock gratitude, "And it's all thanks to you!"

Jill laughed and shook free. "You're so embarrassing. Come on."

They carried on down the street, trying to look as though they weren't sweating from the oppressive heat. Katy glanced nervously down the road.

The van was gone.

She knew she had an overactive imagination — her teachers often lamented how easily distracted she was — but this time, she was *sure* she was onto something. Maybe the van belonged to a Russian spy gathering intel on... what time American schools close on a Friday?

No, that couldn't be right. That was silly.

It was the FBI. It had to be. Bobby Chan once told her he had seen a UFO hovering above the school. The Feds must be here to investigate. Still, Bobby Chan was a weirdo who smelled of pond water. She doubted he would be a reliable source of information.

"Where are you going?" asked Jill.

Katy realized she had passed the entrance to Schofield Lane.

Too preoccupied?

God, even her brain was turning into one of her teachers. She was *definitely* spending too much time at school.

She glanced down the lane. It had rarely looked so

uninviting. Narrower, somehow, the gray buildings on either side stretching to the sky and keeping the sun out.

"Guess I'll see you later," she said, trying to shake the annoying feeling.

"It's a date." Jill stared at her. "You still thinking about that dirty old van?"

"No," said Katy. Then, sheepishly, "Yeah, maybe."

"Want me to walk you home?"

"Huh? Oh, no, it's okay. It spooked me, that's all."

"Then we'll walk together. I don't mind." Jill offered her a lopsided grin. "I love to spend my Fridays strolling through industrial parks, I really do."

Katy shook her head. "I'll be fine, honestly. I'll see you Monday. Unless you wanna go to the movies tomorrow?"

"Sure. Message me. As long as it's not a horror film. I've still not recovered from that last one." Jill squeezed Katy's arm, smiled, and walked on, leaving Katy alone on the street.

She stood a while, the midday sun sizzling on her face. The street was quiet. A few stragglers scuffed their way along, hands in pockets, or engrossed in their phones. She gazed down Schofield Lane and hesitated. What the hell was wrong with her? She had walked down this alley every day for the last two years, ever since her father had acquiesced to her demands and stopped sending a chauffeur to pick her up. She just wanted to be like other girls her age, which was why she didn't go to a private school, or have a personal tutor for maths (though she needed one), or get picked up outside school by a limo. It was embarrassing.

Luckily, her dad had agreed. He agreed to pretty much everything she asked. She had him wrapped around her little finger, that's what her mom used to say, until the accident took her from them. That was five years ago, when Katy was eleven. Her dad had never remarried, and it had been up to him to raise her. Unfortunately, this also meant he had to give her the dreaded 'talks'.

Boys, sex, drugs, alcohol; he had somehow muddled his way through all of them. Katy would never forget — no matter how hard she tried — the time he had sat down next to her on the bed and discussed periods, and the changes to her body, and about becoming a woman, his face growing redder with each spluttering word.

"It's okay, dad. Girls talk," she had said, letting him off the hook. She had never seen relief wash over someone quite as fast as that. It made her smile to think that her dad — one of the biggest producers in Hollywood, the man behind two Oscar-nominated films (*Under the Black Skies of Night* and *Two Women,* both of which Katy thought were boring) — could be reduced to a gibbering wreck with one simple word.

Menstruation.

She supposed all dads were like that, but the idea made it no less amusing.

Feeling better, Katy left the main street and slunk off down the alley, avoiding the broken glass and the dog shit. A light wind whistled after her, swirling candy wrapper butterflies through the air. She only glanced over her shoulder once. Satisfied there was no one following her, she carried on, looking forward to getting home. She would have the house all to herself. The pool cleaner would be gone, and she could spend the rest of the afternoon listening to music and floating in the water. Her homework could wait.

It was a hot, lazy weekend, and she had a feeling it was gonna be a *real* good one.

3

"Shit! She saw us," grunted Baxter. Then, to himself, *"Suddenly she's fucking psychic."* He knew his pathetic ruse of looking in the glove compartment hadn't fooled her for a second.

"You think she knows?" asked Corvo, ducking down into his seat. Baxter looked at him, at the confusion and fear on his round face, a face Baxter had grown to hate over the few months they had known each other.

"Of course not. She's a nosy fucking kid. All those rich bitches think everyone is out to get them and their money."

Corvo resumed tapping his nails nervously against the phone. "So the plan is on?"

"Of course it is. Nothing's changed. We just have to be more careful. Send the message." The van careened around a corner and almost ran a set of red lights. Baxter braked sharply, sending Corvo's phone flying from his hands.

"Fuck," said Corvo, stretching forward, the phone out of reach.

"What are you doing? Send the fucking message!"

Corvo unclasped his seatbelt and groped beneath his feet for the device. "I can't find it!"

"Jesus Christ," muttered Baxter. "Check under the seat."

"I'm trying."

A flurry of car horns snapped Baxter back to reality. The lights had turned green. He wiped sweat from his eyes and accelerated. The van stank of Corvo's BO.

Nice going, asshole, thought Baxter. *Way to draw attention to yourself. So far you've almost hit a car, nearly run some lights and knocked down a pedestrian, then caused mass road rage. What's next? The whole van gonna explode?*

"Found it!" said Corvo, thumping his head off the glove compartment as he sat up.

"Send the message, she'll be there in a minute."

Corvo did as asked.

It was what he did best.

Baxter sighed. Corvo would never be regarded as one of life's great thinkers, but he followed orders and was brutishly strong, and that was all Baxter needed.

Little girls were scared of big, burly men.

He was counting on it.

Jill couldn't enjoy the journey home. She stuffed her headphones in her ears and watched Instagram stories as she walked, but even social media wasn't working for her today. There were only so many unboxings and tips on how to get 'beach body ready' she could take.

Something was gnawing at her. Guilt? Was that it?

She should have accompanied Katy home. She knew it, and Katy undoubtedly knew it too. It was unfair to let her walk by herself after that van had given her a scare.

But wasn't Katy being silly? There was nothing to be afraid of. Or was there? You couldn't be sure these days. There are too many terrible people out there, some walking the streets, others in positions of power, or so her mom always said.

"Damn," said Jill. "I'm a bad friend."

"What's that, honey?" asked a passing old lady.

Jill looked at her, surprised. "Nothing. Just talking to myself."

"That's a sign of old age," said the lady, leaning crookedly on her cane.

Jill smiled, turned, and headed back towards Schofield Lane. If she hurried, she could catch Katy before she reached the industrial park. Then they could spend the afternoon together, readying their beach bodies by eating copious amounts of ice cream and vegging out by the pool before Katy's driver took her home in the limo.

All in all, it was a damn fine plan.

"Excuse me, can you help?"

The voice jolted Katy from her thoughts. She looked for the source and saw a woman standing by a dull green car, the hood propped up.

Katy pointed at herself, somewhat bemused.

The woman nodded, wandering up to her with an appreciative smile. She wore comically large sunglasses that obscured most of her face, but Katy had never understood nor cared for fashion, so she didn't question them.

It was her first mistake.

The woman gestured at the vehicle.

"I'm sorry to ask, but I've been having a bit of car trouble."

Katy offered her an anxious smile. "Sorry, I don't know much about cars. You want me to phone someone?" She wondered why the woman hadn't done that herself. Mind you, adults were funny. Some of them still used pay-as-you-go phone plans and complained about running out of data. She sometimes even saw them in the phone booths dotted around the city, but she wasn't sure they were always using the phone. Peeing, certainly. Doing drugs, almost definitely. Having sex? Probably. Adults are weird.

And also poor, sometimes.

She mentally slapped her own wrist. How narrow-minded of her! She tried never to forget how fortunate she was to not have to worry about money. She hated being rich. It had been thrust upon her purely as a result of being born, and sometimes the guilt weighed heavily on her. Katy ensured her father donated a lot of money to charity every year, and for her own part, she tried to live as frugal a life as the average teenager. Well, except for her birthday. Then all bets were off.

She noticed the woman was looking at her funny and realized she must have asked her a question.

"I'm sorry, what did you say?"

The woman smiled. "A lot on your mind, huh? I remember being your age, just drifting off sometimes. I miss it. Anyway, I said would you mind giving me a push? I think I've fixed the problem, but I can't get the car to start."

Katy laughed. "Me? Push a car?"

The woman grimaced. "Yeah, sorry. There's no one else to ask. This place is a ghost town."

"The offices close at lunchtime on a Friday," said Katy. They looked at each other awkwardly for a moment. "Bad place to break down," she said, trying to fill the silence. "I mean, I suppose there's never a good place to break down. Unless it happened outside a garage. That would be okay. Except at night. Then it would be closed."

You're babbling.

The woman didn't seem to know what to say to that stream-of-consciousness rant, and Katy couldn't blame her. It happened all too frequently.

"So, would you mind?" said the woman, glancing over her shoulder. "Giving me a push, I mean."

Katy looked around for anyone else, but they were alone. It was why she usually enjoyed the walk home, a spot of solitude after a long day at school. Too much socializing tired her out. Since her mom's passing, her dad had become the unofficial party king of Hollywood. Every few weeks he would rent a place in the valley and invite all his movie industry friends over for a wild weekend, and sometimes Katy would be invited too. She had met Tom Cruise and Chris Hemsworth and Scarlett Johansson and all the rest (but not Timothée Chalamet, dammit), and while it had been exciting for a while, she quickly grew weary of it.

"So?" The woman looked at Katy expectantly. "Will you help me?"

"Oh, yeah, sorry," said Katy. She felt her cheeks color. "My dad says I'm a daydreamer. My teachers too."

"It's okay. A good imagination is healthy," said the woman. Katy found her easy-going nature naturally disarming.

"That's what I always say," smiled Katy, and it was true. Whenever her teacher—

"You coming?" asked the woman, snapping Katy from her reverie.

But what if she's a maniac? What if she's come to kill you and—

STOP IT!

She jogged towards the car, short-circuiting her imagination before it fired into overdrive. She couldn't help it. Her brain had always operated like a ball-bearing ricocheting around a pinball machine.

"I can try," she said, shouting the words to be heard over her thoughts. Realizing how obnoxious she sounded, she lowered her voice. "I'm not very strong, though. What if you push, and I start the car?"

"Can you drive?"

"No, but it can't be hard."

You just turn the key and press the accelerator, right?

The woman smiled and put her hand on Katy's shoulder. She was wearing gloves, which struck Katy as odd. "Let's try it my way first, okay?" The smile was warm, reassuring, and Katy let the woman lead her to the car, her hand on the small of Katy's back, guiding her insistently.

Katy felt bad. She was the last person on Earth anyone would pick to push a car. Slender and petite, she didn't exactly have vast reserves of strength to draw on. She doubted she could even move the car an inch, but the lady was so nice, and she was in trouble and needed help, so Katy decided to try her best.

"Just stand here, and when I say, push as hard as you can," said the woman. Katy noticed for the first time that she was wearing a wig, and not a good one. It was the kind you buy in Party City for a Halloween costume, and the woman's natural dark hairline peeked below the seam. Katy tried not to stare. Maybe she was losing her hair, or had cancer, or alopecia, or—

The woman left her and settled herself into the front

seat. A phone pinged loudly. Katy knew it wasn't hers. She kept her iPhone on silent at all times.

"Okay, you ready?" the woman shouted.

Katy gave her a thumbs up, then realized the woman probably couldn't see her.

"Go for it," she called back, bracing herself against the car, planting the heels of her black ankle-boots firmly on the ground, as if that would make any difference. She heard a noise behind her, the screech of tires on gravel. The woman gunned the engine. It spluttered and died. Katy turned and saw a vehicle approaching.

A white van.

A chill skated down her spine. Something wasn't right.

"Try again," called the woman from the front seat, but Katy was already backing away.

Too many coincidences, too many odd details.

See, you should listen to me, said a voice in her head.

Shut up, brain.

"There's someone coming, maybe they can help," she said, pointing to the approaching vehicle, failing to hide the tremor in her voice.

"Hey, wait," said the woman. The car door burst open and she got out, following Katy, trying to act normal but walking too quickly, too quickly by far. The van raced towards them.

"Sorry, I have to go," said Katy, gesturing behind her. She turned, breaking into a jog, and suddenly the woman was right there, tugging on her school bag. "Stop," she tried to say, but the woman pulled hard, knocking her off-balance, and Katy fell to the concrete, landing on her ass.

The woman was on her in a flash, covering her mouth, muffling her screams. Her arm snaked around Katy's torso as the white van screeched to a halt. The doors opened and two men in ski masks leaped out, one of them skidding on the loose stones and crashing to the ground. The other raced towards her and the woman. Katy doubted he was coming to her aid.

She kicked out at him as he approached, but he caught her leg effortlessly, his hands wrapping around her ankle like a python. Together, they lifted her, hustling her towards the van. She struggled, but she was powerless against the two adults.

The third person — she could tell it was a man, he was built like a tank — picked himself up off the ground and ran to the back of the van, throwing the doors open, his eyes darting skittishly around.

Katy wanted to scream, but the woman's hand covered her mouth. She tried to bite her, succeeding only in biting down on the inside of her own cheeks.

"Come on," grunted the man that held her, one leg tucked under each of his arms. He could see up her skirt, and though she knew it wasn't important right now, she felt inexplicably humiliated, flashing back to that time she had come out of the washroom with her skirt tucked into her underwear and everyone had laughed at her.

Focus, you idiot!

They were almost at the van. She was running out of time. Once they had her inside, there would be no one to save her. They could do... whatever they wanted to do to her. In a panic, she bucked her body, loosening one leg from the man's grip. Without hesitation, she kicked him in the throat.

"Fuck," he choked, letting her legs drop to the ground. He paused a second, and she saw the intense, burning hatred in his eyes. "Bitch," he snarled, then punched her hard in the stomach. Katy wheezed as he knocked the air out of her. She tried to double over, but the woman had too tight a grip on her.

"Put her in the van and let's go," said the woman.

The man glared at Katy through narrowed eyes. His hands tightened into fists. She thought he was about to hit her again, and braced herself for impact. Then a voice rang out, echoing across the industrial park.

"Katy!"

Everyone froze, like some bored god had hit pause so he could go take a leak and not miss any of the drama.

Katy turned towards the sound, that achingly familiar voice she knew and loved.

Jill stood at the end of the lane, rooted to the spot. Her eyes were wide, her face ashen and afraid. Katy took her chance. She wrenched her head free from the woman's grip and screamed.

"Run! Call the cops!"

Katy saw the panicked look in the eyes of the man in the ski mask. "Fuck," he said. Time slowed, like a scene from one of her father's beloved westerns, everyone waiting for someone else to make the first move.

The man's eyes darted from herself to Jill and back again. She felt the woman's hand tighten over her mouth, pinching her nose and making it hard to breathe. She saw the bigger man, the one by the open doors of the van, start to move.

But the last thing Katy saw was Jill spinning on her heels and running back down the alleyway, before the man in the ski mask punched her in the side of the head and her body went limp. She was vaguely aware of being dragged over the gravel, and had the ridiculous thought that her dad would be annoyed at her scuffed boots, and then she was inside the van.

As Katy swam in and out of consciousness, she said a silent prayer for Jill.

Then the van doors slammed shut and everything went dark.

~

Jill had stood still for too long. This was something she had never felt before.

Terror.

Real, bone-chilling *terror*. Her stomach was a void, her own legs betraying her desire to run. But run where? To help her friend? Or herself?

There was little time to consider her options.

What good could she do against those people... those *kidnappers*? For that's what they were, surely? Or were they planning on taking Katy somewhere, doing obscene things to her, and leaving her body in a ditch?

The idea appalled her, and she felt an overwhelming urge to cry.

Run, Katy had shouted. *Call the cops.*

It was good advice. Everything rested on her shoulders now. Katy's life... and perhaps her own. A huge man in a black ski mask came racing towards her like an angry gorilla. *He* hadn't hesitated.

She turned and ran back down the alley. It had never looked longer. Her bag slipped off her shoulders as she hurtled towards the safety of the main road, the tall build-ings on either side looming over her like thunderous giants closing in for the kill. Behind her, the man kept pace. She dodged a trashcan, grazing it with her thigh. Seconds later, it smashed off the wall as the man shoved it aside. Every step he took seemed to narrow the gap. She looked back to check how near he was. He was close.

Very close indeed.

Panic set in, that breathless feeling returning, an aching in her lungs that impeded her progress. She turned her head, a second too late to see the stack of empty crates. She hit them running. They crashed to the ground with her, tumbling over her prone body, catching on her tangled limbs. She tried to fight her way through, but it was useless. A hand clamped over her mouth, and the man grabbed her waist, lifting her from the ground. Her legs kicked harmlessly at thin air.

Cars shot by ahead of her. She was so close to the end of the alley, to the main street. A bus pulled up, caught at the lights, and for a brief moment she could see several people, all of them with their heads down, staring at their phone screens in dazed rapture. She wrestled one hand free and frantically waved it, desperate to capture someone's attention, as the man lugged her back towards the van. A small blonde girl watched her from the bus window. She tugged on her mother's sleeve, pointing at Jill, but the woman brushed her hand away, and then the bus was moving, the little girl waving sadly from the window until she was out of sight.

"Stop struggling," said the man. "You weren't meant to be here."

They were out of the lane now, the desolate buildings of the industrial park surrounding them. The man clutched her too tight, bundling her into the van. Another man was already in there with Katy. He raised his fist.

Tears stung Jill's eyes.

She was surprised they hadn't come sooner.

4

———

Katy lay still. What sense was there in struggling? She couldn't overpower one adult, never mind three. Better to conserve her strength. She might need it. She didn't know what they had planned.

Someone — she thought it was the woman — tied her wrists behind her back.

"Ow," she yelped as the knot pulled taut, chafing her skin. She received a smack on the back of her head in response. It wasn't sore, not like when the man had punched her. Jeez, she hadn't been punched in years, not since she had argued with Louisa Black about which of them had the longest hair.

"Shut up, and you might get through this," said a man's voice, muffled by his ski mask. The woman tied Katy's ankles together, then pulled a filthy rag over her eyes, almost tight enough to bisect her skull. The van turned a sharp corner, and Katy slid helplessly across the floor, bumping into Jill.

Poor Jill.

One of the men had hit her in the face, and she hadn't

moved since. Was she... dead?

And if she is, does that mean it's your fault?

No! She couldn't think that.

"We did it. We got her," said a low, guttural voice from the front of the van.

"Oh yeah," said the woman. "That went without a hitch. Except now we've got two of them. What the fuck are we gonna do with *her?*"

"Yeah, Bax," said the other man. He sounded on edge. "You said there'd only be one. You said, man, you said you'd done your research."

"Shut up," replied the driver.

Bax. The one driving is called Bax. Baxter?

Obviously. What do you think it stands for, Baximillion?

His voice was calm. Katy figured him for the leader.

She filed the information away. Anything could come in useful. So far, she hadn't seen anyone's face properly. The woman had been wearing sunglasses and a wig, the men ski masks.

It wasn't enough to identify anyone.

That was good. If she didn't see their faces, there was less chance they would kill her. Though the fact they were saying their names out loud alarmed her.

Please let those be fake names. Please.

"It changes nothing," said the driver, the one known as Bax. "We have the prize, and that's what matters. So we came away with a little extra. Who cares? Maybe *her* dad's rich too. We might've lucked out."

"I dunno, man. I don't like this." The other man was nervous, and she figured this was his first real criminal act, probably only in it for the money.

Hey, I'm pretty good at this.

Except you don't know if any of it is true.

"I don't give a shit what you like," snapped the woman. "I'm not in this to make friends. Once we're through, I'll happily never see either of you shit-heels again."

They stopped talking for a while, the hum of the engine taking over. It sent vibrations coursing throughout Katy's body, and every so often the vehicle would judder over a bump and she would smack her forehead off the cold, hard floor. She had to say something, reason with them. But what? What could she possibly say to make them change their minds?

Maybe her dad's rich too.

That's what the woman had said. So it was a kidnapping. A ransom. Now it all made sense. If they wanted to kill someone, they could have gotten any girl off the street.

Yeah, you keep telling yourself that.

She swallowed hard, and then, in her most grown-up voice, said, "Please let us go. We won't tell anyone. I promise."

The nervous man laughed. "*I promise,*" he repeated in a mocking tone. He chuckled again, but there was no sincerity in it, as if he was laughing for his own benefit to prove he wasn't afraid.

He's the weak link, she thought. But what did that mean? How was that information useful?

"Just shut up," said the woman, "and hope your daddy is willing to splash the cash. You never know, you might get out of this in one piece. You *and* your friend."

Katy fell silent. There was no point arguing, not right now. They were all high on adrenaline, and she wouldn't be able to change their minds, not as a group.

It was like what her dad always said about social media. He insisted that arguing online was a waste of time.

You can only hope to enact change on an individual, face-to-face basis, he said.

But she also knew that her dad had a second Facebook account where he responded to criticism of his movies under the alias Roger White, a thirty-four-year-old law school graduate with two kids and a condo in Barbados, so her dad was also full of shit. Still, what he had told her made sense.

She had to get them alone.

And do what? What are you talking about?

She would know when the time came, and right now, she had plenty of time to think.

The van rumbled along for what felt like hours. Unable to see anything, Katy listened. The noise of the traffic had steadily decreased until only the occasional passing car was audible. The sound the wheels made had also changed, from a typical tarmac screech to rougher terrain, a dirt track, maybe even off-road. There were more bumps, the worst ones sending her an inch off the ground before slamming her back to Earth.

At that moment, she truly hated gravity. What good was it, anyway? Without gravity, everyone could fly around wherever they wanted. It would be so cool. She would never have to take the elevator again, not when she could just float up the side of the building and knock on her dad's window.

Concentrate, Katy.

She tried, reluctantly giving up on the fantasy of somersaulting through the air across an entire basketball court to perform a slam dunk, the whole school cheering her name.

Instead, she listened.

For what? Clues?

Yeah. Why not? There was nothing else to do, and the gang made it easy, using their names with reckless abandon.

The nervous man — the one in the back with her — was called Corvo. It was an unusual name, and it suggested that perhaps they *were* using codenames. That, or they were totally incompetent.

She hoped it was the former.

Somehow, it seemed safer to be kidnapped by professionals, people who had done this before and would do so again. They were less likely to kill her. A group of bungling criminals would be more inclined to mess up and make a mistake, one that could cost Katy her life.

And Jill. Don't forget Jill.

She knew Jill was still alive. In the quieter moments, if she listened closely, she could hear her friend breathing softly over the rumble of the engine. It was a beautiful sound. Never again would she complain about Jill's snoring keeping her awake during their sleepovers.

She had been right about Bax. His name was short for Baxter, which reminded her of a joke James McAvoy had told her at one of her father's soirées.

What's ET short for?

Because he's got wee legs!

She hadn't understood it at the time, and had asked her dad. "Scottish humor," he had replied with a shrug.

Katy, for god's sake, focus!

She was trying to.

The nervous man — Corvo — had talked about a plan, about research. Had they been following her, watching her? And for how long? The thought disgusted her. Not so much for the voyeuristic intrusion, but for the fact she had been unaware. How could a man watch her for that long without her noticing? Was she so wrapped up in her own life?

No, she couldn't — *wouldn't* — blame herself.

The van jerked to a halt, and she slid into Jill again.

They had arrived.

"Alright," said Baxter from the front seat. "Unload the package." His voice was clearer now. Katy suspected he had removed the ski mask. It made sense — there was nothing more suspicious than a man in a ski mask driving a van during the height of summer.

"What package?" asked Corvo.

"The fucking girls, you asshole."

"You want them in the cellar?"

"Jesus, you gonna give them our GPS signal next? Just get them out of here, you dumb fuck. I'll get Varg to help you."

Varg? Who was that? Another member of the gang? How many *were* there?

The van doors loudly opened. Katy felt Corvo's beefy hands on her ankles, dragging her backwards towards the exit with little regard for her comfort. He rolled her onto her back, then lifted her into a sitting position. She had a moment to breathe before the big man hefted her onto his shoulder, carrying her like a slab of meat.

That's all you are to him.

He placed one hand on her butt to steady her, and Katy couldn't help herself.

"Let go," she said, and to her astonishment, he moved his hand to her lower back.

"Sorry," he whispered.

Hey, it's got manners.

She took the opportunity to listen again. There were no honking horns, no buzzing engines, no music bleeding from open windows. Instead, water lapped at a shore. Gulls cawed, their cries carried on the mournful wind. She could smell the sea. Was she at the beach? It was a four hour drive from her school, so it was certainly possible. The salty air tickled her nostrils, and she pictured herself as a kid at the amusement park with her parents, wolfing down cotton candy and crying while waiting in line for the rollercoaster.

She noticed Corvo's footsteps made no sound, and figured it was due to the sand. That, or he was a ghost, but honestly, the whole sandy beach thing made more sense.

"That her?" said a new voice. "That the bitch that's gonna make me rich?" The words were slurred, drunken. It had to be the man Baxter had called Varg.

"Yeah," said Corvo. "There's another in the van."

"That's what Baxter said. I thought he was yanking my chain. Why've we got two of 'em?"

"It's her friend."

"A witness?" said Varg, and Katy hated the way he said it.

The word 'witness' carried dreadful implications. She knew what happened to witnesses. One of her father's films, *A Witness to Murder*, had been about a woman hunted by the mafia for witnessing a gang slaying. Her dad had forbidden her from watching it until she was seventeen — it was one of his few R-rated films — but she and Jill had snuck a copy out of his study and watched it one night. The things they did to that woman when they caught her... they had tortured her, stripped her, abused her... she could under-stand why she wasn't allowed to watch it. In the end, of course, she was rescued by the police, led by the heroic alco-holic cop played by Adam Sandler, of all people. She remembered her disappointment at the ending, wishing that the woman had fought back and killed the bad guys herself. She told Jill that's what *she* would have done.

So what're you waiting for? Now's your big chance.

As if.

The man she assumed was Varg moved closer, blocking

the small amount of light that crept in through the blind-fold. The sea-air was replaced by hideous bad-breath.

"You smell real nice, girly," he said. "Wonder if you taste as good as you smell."

"*Varg,*" shouted Baxter from somewhere behind them. "*Quit flirting and get the other one.*"

"Later, girly," he whispered, his breath hot on her ear, his dry lips making brief contact, and then she was off again, carried by Corvo, grateful to be away from this Varg guy. She heard Corvo kick open a door. The wind stopped, his feet pounding on wooden flooring, then onto what sounded like kitchen linoleum, the soles of his shoes slurping against the sticky floor. Her shoulder bumped against a doorframe, and then Corvo was treading on wooden floorboards again. A key rattled in a lock.

"Shit," mumbled Corvo. "Which key is it?"

He tried several before finding the right one. The door creaked open. They bounced down a set of stairs, the steps groaning like hungry wolves. The air was warm, the smell of damp wood lingering. When they reached the bottom of the stairs, Corvo gently deposited Katy onto something soft. A mattress?

My, how thoughtful.

She lay still, hearing his joints pop as he kneeled by her.

"Listen," he said, "Don't cause trouble, don't try to escape, and you'll get home safe."

"Why are you doing this?" she asked softly.

"Just do what they say, okay? And don't ask questions." He stood, then added, "I don't wanna have to hurt you."

And then she was alone. She lay a while, ankles still tied, wrists bound behind her back. She wiped her ear against the mattress, trying to remove the saliva Varg had left there.

He scared her. The others, not so much. It was the way he had spoken to her.

Girly.

She felt sick.

Wonder if you taste as good as you smell.

Let him try it. She'd kill him. Or maybe she'd escape and hunt him down, like the woman should have done in *A Witness to Murder*. Then she could tell her dad all about it, and he could make a sequel, starring herself.

Would you take this fucking seriously? This isn't one of your stupid daydreams.

But her imagination was running wild. She would shoot him in the chest, let him bleed out slowly... no, she would shoot him in his... in his *penis*. Yes, that would show him!

He'll be back, you know.

She knew. By then, she would already be free.

She shuffled to the edge of the mattress and pressed her face to the seam, working the rag away from her eyes.

Wait.

She had to be careful. Varg would arrive shortly with Jill. If she managed to get the blindfold off, he would simply retie it. No, she had to think this through, and not make any rash decisions.

Her life — and that of her best friend — depended on it.

5

———

TIME PASSED IN DRACONIAN SILENCE.

Every so often — it could have been seconds, could have been hours — Katy called Jill's name, but so far there had been no response. Varg had dumped her friend on the mattress next to her, lingering an uncomfortably long time before Baxter came to get him. She tried not to think of what Varg had been up to, alone in the dark with the unconscious Jill.

"Hey," she said, eager to hear a voice, even if it was her own. "Jill."

The girl stirred, but did not wake, and Katy turned her attention once more to the blindfold. She rubbed her face against the mattress, trying to work it up and off her eyes. It was no use. She needed her friend.

"Jill, wake up," she hissed.

"Hmmmmph," replied Jill. It wasn't much, but it was a start.

Katy nudged her with her head. Jill rolled away from her.

"Stop it, mommy."

Katy giggled. *"Mommy?"*

"It's not a school day," she said sleepily.

"Jesus, Jill, it's me. It's Katy. Wake up!"

"Huh? Where are—" She tried to sit, and found she couldn't. "What's happening?"

"It's going to be okay," said Katy.

"Okay? I can't move! Katy, I can't move!"

"I know. We've... we've been kidnapped."

The words sounded absurd.

"What?" said Jill, her breath coming in tight gasps. "That's not possible. *I can't move!*"

"Neither can I. Just try not to panic, it'll only make the ropes tighter."

"Panic? *Panic?* Oh god. *Oh god! Help! Help!*" shrieked Jill.

Katy let her scream for a little while. When she finally ran out of steam, Katy put her face close to her friend's.

"Jill, listen to me. There's no one around. We're in the middle of nowhere, and the only people who can hear you are the kidnappers."

Jill started to cry. "Are they going to kill us?"

"No," said Katy. "They're going to ask for a ransom."

"But my parents aren't rich. They can't..." She trailed off as the realization dawned on her. Katy kept quiet. "They didn't want me, did they?" said Jill.

"No," said Katy in a small voice. She didn't know what else to say.

Jill wept. "They're going to kill me."

Katy knew she had to do something. She had to change the subject, set Jill at ease, stop her crying, make her believe everything was going to—

"Do you like pancakes?" she blurted out. She winced internally. Was that the best she could come up with?

And yet somehow it worked.

"What?" said Jill. She sniffed, turning in Katy's direction. "You… you know I do."

"I know," said Katy. "I just wanted to get your attention."

Jill was quiet for a moment. "So you asked me about pancakes?"

"It was the first thing that came to mind."

"We've been kidnapped, and the first thing that came to mind was *pancakes?*"

"I think I'm hungry," said Katy, and Jill laughed at that. It wasn't her normal, sweet laugh — there was an undercurrent of fear — but it was better than her sobbing.

Quick, you've calmed her down!

Katy snuggled up to her friend. "Can you get my blindfold off?"

"My hands are tied."

"Use your teeth. Here," said Katy, pushing her face against Jill's mouth. The girl bit down on the rag, then recoiled in horror.

"Oh god, it tastes disgusting."

"That's what you're worried about?" snapped Katy. For a second, she thought Jill might cry again. Then she felt her friend's breath on her face as Jill fastened her teeth over the blindfold, her nose squeezing against Katy's forehead as she tugged the fabric down.

"That's it," said Katy. "You did it."

Jill sniffed. "I… I did it."

It was a small victory, but under the current circumstances, one worth celebrating.

"That's right," said Katy. "We're gonna get through this. *Together.*"

Jill broke down again, great gulping sobs wracking her body. Katy lay beside her and kissed her gently on the forehead. Her skin tasted salty.

"Who are they?" asked Jill.

"I don't know. There're four of them. Baxter, Emma, Corvo, and Varg."

"How do you know their names?"

"I've been listening. I think Baxter is the leader, or maybe Emma. He acts like he's in charge, but I'm not so sure, because Emma sounds like Ms. Keller."

"Our maths teacher?" said Jill. "You think it's her?"

"Are you serious? Of course not."

God, Jill could be such a dope sometimes.

"You always said she doesn't like you."

"Jill, we've not been kidnapped by our math teacher."

"But..."

"What's she gonna do, hold us to ransom for my trigonometry homework?"

Jill started to cry again.

"I'm sorry," said Katy. She hated apologizing to Jill, especially when she was acting like an idiot, but felt she had to.

"It's okay," whispered Jill.

Crisis averted.

"What was I saying?"

Jill sniffed. "You were telling me about the kidnappers."

"Oh, yeah. So, Corvo is the guy who chased you down the lane. He kinda sounds like he doesn't want to be here. He even said sorry when he touched my butt. He's—"

"He touched your butt?"

Katy tried not to get angry at Jill's interruptions.

"It was an accident. I think. Would you just listen? I think Corvo is our best chance."

"Our best chance at what?" said Jill. She sounded both annoyed and confused.

"Escape," said Katy, as if the answer was obvious. To her, it *was*.

"What do you mean? We can't escape. There are three maniacs up there, and—"

"Four. Don't forget about the other man. Varg. I don't know much about him. He wasn't in the van."

Jill was silent for a moment. Then she said, "Oh god, we're going to die in here."

Typical Jill. She was always so dramatic.

"Not if we escape," said Katy. "Don't worry, I'll get us out of here."

Jill tried to roll onto her back, but her bound hands prevented her. She let out an exhausted sigh.

"Katy... don't be stupid. There's no way out."

"Not with *that* attitude."

"Are you joking?"

Katy tried to shrug. "They're not going to hurt us. Why would they? They need us alive. And anyway, we have the element of surprise. They won't expect us to run. They think we're two scared little girls."

"And they're right."

"Come on," urged Katy. "We have to *try.*"

"But what if they chop off our fingers and send them in the mail?"

"No one does that anymore." She shook her head. "No one's done that for, like, a hundred years."

Jill didn't reply, and Katy took the opportunity to look around the cellar. It was pitch black, but as her eyes slowly adjusted, she could make out details.

Wooden steps led up to a door outlined by thin shafts of light. A couple of burlap sacks lay slumped the corner. She could see a small window near the ceiling, but it was boarded up. There were shelves along one wall, and what looked like long thin poles leaning against them. Fishing rods? They *were* by the sea, so she supposed that made sense. She looked up at the ceiling. At first it appeared to be curved, but as her vision improved, she realized it was a large fishing net suspended from the roof.

Okay, so there wasn't much she could do with fishing rods, but if there was a harpoon, or a hunting knife, or...

Doubtful. The gang would have removed any dangerous weaponry prior to the kidnapping.

Probably.

"How are you okay with this?" asked Jill quietly.

Katy almost laughed. "I'm not. I'm scared too, I really am. But don't you think it's kinda exciting?"

"I don't think dying's exciting."

"We're *not* gonna die. We can either wait a few days until my dad pays up, or we can escape and be heroes."

"Katy, this isn't one of your dad's films. This is real life."

"Which is why they won't expect us to escape."

Jill sighed. "Fine, have it your way. As usual."

Katy almost took the bait, but bit her tongue. She knew what Jill was getting at. When Katy got a plan in her head, she would bulldoze through anything — and anyone — in her way, no matter how hare-brained the scheme. But this wasn't like the time she had convinced Jill to join the cheerleading squad so she could make friends with Lucy Eisenberg, or the time they tried to break into school to steal the English test papers. This was serious. She had to remember that.

Oh, shut up. What's the worst that could happen?

"Hey," said Katy, an idea forming. "You have your phone?"

"No, it's in my bag."

"And where's your bag?"

"I... I don't know. Wait, no, I dropped it when they chased me through the lane. What about you?"

"Mine's in my bag too. It's still in the van, unless they've moved it."

They lapsed into thoughtful silence again.

"Where are we?" asked Jill after a while.

"Somewhere by the sea. You hear the waves?"

"I don't hear anything."

Katy's fists tightened into balls.

Well, if you'd just shut up for a second...

"I think we're at a holiday lodge for fishermen or something," she said. "There are rods and nets and..." she struggled to find the right words, settling on "... fishing stuff."

For the first time since they arrived, Jill's face threatened to break into a smile. "How are you so good at this?"

"At what?"

"At being kidnapped?"

Katy laughed softly. "When I told my dad I wanted to go to a normal school, he made me learn about what to do in situations like... like *this*, I guess. What to look for, ways to figure out where you are."

"My god."

"Yeah. I thought it was dumb at the time. Stupid, overprotective dad." She thought of him, and a shiver passed through her body. "We just have to do what they say. Give them as few problems as we can until we escape. Don't make them angry. That's when they might..."

Don't say it.

"Might what?" asked Jill.

Katy clenched her jaw.

That's when they might hurt us. Isn't that what you were going to say?

It was, but it would do no good to say that in front of Jill. She had to be the strong one.

She had to get them out of here.

6

———

"So what now?" asked Emma.

Baxter eyed her warily. "Now," he said, stretching languorously, "We wait."

The four of them were gathered in the kitchen of the disused beach house. It was the perfect base of operations, as Baxter knew it would be. He had chosen it for the isolation. Their nearest neighbors were seven miles away, the nearest main road twenty-four. Most importantly, there was a cellar, electricity, and gas. For now, they would call it home.

Until the money came. The big score. Twenty million dollars in cash, enough to set them up for life.

Baxter smiled to himself. It was all too easy.

Snatch the bitch, collect the dough, return her in nearly-new condition.

Simple as that.

"Don't we have to tell someone we've got her?" said Corvo in his insipid voice.

"Do you never listen, you fucking potato?" growled Baxter. "We've gone over this. We wait a day, *then* make the call. Let that rich fucker sweat a little. Get him on the edge. Then, we strike. He'll be so relieved, he'll do *anything* to get her back. Money's no object to fucks like him."

"By then he'll have called the cops," said Emma.

"But they won't have tapped the line, not if they don't know it's a kidnapping."

Varg took a swig from his hip-flask. "What else could it be?"

Baxter glanced at him, then went back to cleaning his nails with his switchblade. If Corvo was bad, Varg was worse. He was a danger. To Baxter, to the girls, and to everyone around him. Obnoxious, untrustworthy, and most likely a sexual degenerate, he was only here because he was friends with Corvo, and Baxter thought his intimidating presence might come in handy. Now that he knew how easy it was to kidnap a couple of girls, he realized he didn't need Varg.

Too late, asshole. You're stuck with him.

"They might think she's run off with her boyfriend," said Emma, answering Varg's question, for which Baxter was thankful. He didn't even like looking at the man, never mind talking to him. He was perpetually unwashed, his thinning, greasy hair sagging across his lined, hard face. For the last three weeks, he had worn the same black t-shirt with some heavy metal band on it, the logo an incomprehensible squiggle. Varg had told him it said Burzum, who were apparently true Norwegian black metal, whatever the fuck *that* meant. Baxter wondered if they had anything to do with the swastika tattoo on Varg's neck, currently hidden by his straggly beard.

"I'll be her boyfriend," said Varg, taking a long drink.

"You ain't gonna touch her," said Baxter. How many fucking times did he—

"What about her little friend? She wasn't part of the deal."

"You can't touch either of them!" shouted Baxter. "We're a professional operation here, not a bunch of fucking rapists. And stop drinking so much, we need everyone alert."

Varg took another drink, nice and slow. If he was doing it to piss Baxter off, he had achieved the desired effect.

"Alert for what?" said Varg. "No one knows we're here, and those two girlies ain't gonna escape. They'll be too busy pissing their little panties in fear."

Baxter shook his head and turned to Emma.

"So, as I was saying, we call tomorrow. 12pm sharp. Let's really fuck up his lunch."

"Twenty million in unmarked bills," said Emma.

Corvo cleared his throat, and they looked in his direction. He stared at his feet, shuffled them.

"Uh, Bax... when you phone him, you gonna ask about the other thing, yeah?"

"What *other* thing?" said Baxter, his patience wearing thin.

"You know, the thing we spoke about."

"I have no idea what—"

"Remaking *The Last Jedi*. Remember we spoke about it? That night in the club? You said we'd make that one of our demands."

"I'm not gonna do that," said Baxter, failing to hide the irritation in his voice.

"It's perfect though," said Corvo. "We ask for the money, and demand they redo the movie. We're the only people in a position to do this. I mean, it's the Skywalker saga, it's Luke's story, and he's—"

"*I'm not gonna fucking do it!*" exploded Baxter. He put his head in his hands, feeling his blood pressure rising. "I don't give a shit about *Star Wars*, or *Star Trek,* or... or..."

"Game of Thrones?" said Varg, smiling to himself, screwing and unscrewing the cap on his hip flask.

"Exactly," said Baxter. "We kidnap a girl, and all this bastard wants to talk about is remaking fucking *Star Wars*. Jesus Christ." He sighed. "No reward is worth this."

Corvo thumped his fist off the table. "That's a fucking line from the movie, man! That's Han Solo! You did that deliberately." He stood, towering over Baxter, the veins in his neck and biceps bulging obscenely.

"Sit down," said Emma. "I don't want to hear another word about fucking *Star Wars*. We wait. That's all. One of us stays awake, keeps watch, and tomorrow we call Kevin Ketcher and get our money. Until then, everyone just stay cool."

Corvo lurched back into his seat like a scolded child.

"I'm gonna go piss," said Baxter, heading for the door. He could only take so much of their fucking shenanigans.

"May the force be with you," said Varg, and if Baxter had been armed, he would have shot him dead there and then.

7

———

They had lain in silence for a long time.

The full gravity of the situation kept threatening to overwhelm Katy, but whenever it reared its snake-like head, she forced the feeling down.

Back when her father had instructed her on what to do in a kidnap scenario, she had gone to bed every night fantasizing about it. In her head, she had been cool under pressure, relaxing her muscles to slip free of her bonds. Then, she had found an air vent, unscrewed the bolts with a convenient nail file, and climbed through the narrow metal tunnel, ignoring the rats and spiders, before vanishing into the night, leaving the kidnappers scratching their heads in frustration.

If only it were that easy.

She was giving herself a headache, and rolled over to look at Jill. Katy felt a vicious stab of regret. If not for her, Jill would be safely home watching Netflix.

"Why'd you come back for me?" she asked. Her voice shattered the quiet, sounding insanely loud in the dingy cellar.

"I didn't want you to think I was a bad friend," was Jill's reply, and that made Katy feel worse.

"I'd never think that. You're my best friend."

"But I left you. You were scared, and I *left* you."

"But you came back for me." Katy paused. "Bet you wish you hadn't."

"That's not funny," said Jill, but she laughed anyway.

Katy loved Jill's laugh. It was the kind of infectious giggle that always made her smile.

"Jill?" she said.

"Yeah?"

"I want you to know, there's no one I'd rather be kidnapped with."

"What about Tom Holland?"

"You're right," said Katy. "There's only one person I'd rather be kidnapped with."

But the moment had passed, and grim reality encroached once more. After a while, Katy spoke.

"We need to get out of here."

"Shouldn't we wait?"

"You think that's a good idea?"

"I prefer it to getting killed."

It was sound logic. Typical Jill! Katy tried a different tactic.

"What if," she said, thinking of how best to word it, not wanting to frighten Jill *too* much, "What if once they get the money, they kill us anyway? Or maybe they leave us here and don't tell anyone?"

"Stop it."

"Sorry, but we have to consider it. There must be a way out. That window's high up, but it probably opens right onto the sand. I think we could bust the boards off."

"How? We're tied up."

It was true. Katy was getting ahead of herself.

"Okay then, let's break the plan into phases. Phase one, we untie ourselves."

"That's your plan?"

"I'm still thinking. There're two of us here, you know? I'm open to suggestions."

Katy scanned the room. In a perverse way, she was beginning to enjoy herself. Not the situation, of course — she really needed to pee — but the problem solving. It was like a giant puzzle, or one of those escape rooms. There had to be a way out. She just had to figure it out.

"You sure you can't untie my knots?"

"As sure as you were that you couldn't untie mine."

"Good point," agreed Katy. "We need something to cut them with. Can you see any nails, or pieces of glass?"

"What about a spring from the mattress?"

"But we'd need to cut the mattress to get to them."

"Oh yeah."

"Hey," said Katy, trying to keep Jill as buoyant as she felt. "Remember what Mr. Jefferson used to say in English Lit? There are no wrong answers in a brainstorming session."

"Ugh, I hate that guy. Why is one ear so much bigger than the other?"

"Focus, Jill," said Katy, though she too often wondered the same thing. It wasn't just a bit bigger either, it was literally twice the—

"Shit!"

Jill rolled to face her. "What?"

"That shelf," she said, gesturing with her head towards the wall behind Jill. "There's a bottle."

"What kind?"

"What does is matter? It's a glass one, okay?"

Jill rolled onto her side. "I see it!"

Katy shuffled into a sitting position. Her whole body was numb.

"We need to get that bottle," she said. "How high is the shelf? Think you could reach it?"

"Why me?"

"You're taller than me," said Katy. "You've got a long neck."

Jill turned to her. "Excuse me? What's wrong with my neck?"

"Nothing's *wrong* with it. It's just... it's quite long."

"You've never mentioned that before."

"It's never been relevant."

"So why bring it up now?"

Katy giggled. "Because we need to reach that bottle, and you've got an extra two or three inches on me."

"Two or three inches?"

"Look, you gonna get that bottle or not?"

Jill said nothing. The silent treatment. Katy knew she had gone too far. But dammit, sometimes she couldn't help herself.

"Jill. You've got a lovely neck, I swear."

The girl muttered something.

"What?" said Katy.

Jill turned to her. "I said, how long *is* it?"

"Not long, honestly. It's totally normal. A really normal, pretty neck."

"Now you're just being weird," said Jill.

"Plus, if we're ever stuck on an African plain, you'll have the last laugh when I can't reach those high leaves with you and the other giraffes."

"Katy, I swear—"

"Come on! We can't spend all day talking about your freaky long neck. Get the bottle."

"Fine," snapped Jill. "But when we get home, I'm gonna have to sit you down and talk to you about your big fat ass."

Katy bristled. "I don't have a—" She stopped herself. This was not the time. She took a deep breath. "Look, are you ready or not?"

"Sure thing, fat ass," said Jill. "Now help me up."

"How?"

"Sit up and lean against me. I'll do the same."

Katy did. She struggled round until she had her back to her friend.

"Okay," said Jill. "Push."

They pressed their spines together, both rising at the same time like a pathetic circus act. Katy's legs wobbled, but it seemed to be working. Eventually, Jill hopped to her feet with a grunt, and Katy fell backwards onto the mattress.

"We did it!" said Jill. She smiled down at Katy. "And all thanks to your fat ass."

Katy looked up at her. "Sorry, what did you say? I can't hear you all the way up there."

Jill ignored her. She stood, swaying slightly. Her hands twitched with nerves.

"Take your time," said Katy. "You got this."

Jill swallowed hard. "If I fall over, I'm not sure I can get back up again."

Katy had run out of reassuring platitudes. "You'll be fine," she said, watching as Jill scuffed forwards, moving less than an inch at a time. Still, it was safer than hopping. This way, her feet never left the ground.

It wasn't until Jill was halfway across the cellar floor that she turned to Katy and said, "What if they check on us?"

Katy was quiet. In her enthusiasm, she hadn't considered this.

"Then you'd better be quick," she said.

Some questions are better left unanswered, her dad used to say. She briefly wondered whether they had tried to contact him yet. It seemed unlikely, as he would demand to speak to her, to hear that she was okay.

That she was *alive.*

She knew how bullish her father could be. Hell, he didn't get to be the biggest producer in Hollywood — *second biggest,* he always corrected her — by being shy and retiring.

There's too much of myself in you, he sometimes told her. *Why can't you be more like your mother?*

It was said in jest, but not without truth.

"Okay, I'm almost there," said Jill, snapping Katy back to reality.

"Can you reach?"

The shelf was level with Jill's shoulders. She stared at the empty glass bottle.

"How am I supposed to carry it? My hands are tied."

"Use your mouth."

"That's gross! It's probably been sitting here forever. What if there's a spider inside?"

"Maybe he'll grant us three wishes?"

Just imagine!

What would her wishes be? Well, number one would be for a smaller ass, if what Jill had said was true.

She's just messing with you.

Yeah, she *knew* that. But still...

Okay, so a smaller ass. That was wish one out of the way. Now, wish two. What about invisibility, or—

"Oh god," said Jill, and Katy froze, a new ice age forming

in her blood. In the semi-darkness, she could see her friend, the look of shock and fear on her face. They could both hear it.

The sound of footsteps striding towards the cellar door.

Someone was coming.

8

———

"WHAT DO I DO?"

The steps were getting louder, moving with purpose.

"Stay still," said Katy. It was bad advice, but she had no better suggestions.

What the hell were they doing? Why hadn't they waited?

Because you wanted to be a hero, said the voice in Katy's head. *How does it feel knowing you just got your friend killed?*

"It's gonna be fine," she said, partly to Jill, but mostly to herself.

Please be fine oh please be fine.

The slivers of light surrounding the doorway momentarily darkened as a shadowy figure strode past, then lightened again. The steps continued down the hallway, then a door slammed and all was still.

"Oh my god," said Jill. Katy could tell she was on the verge of tears again. "I'm coming back."

"No! You've made it that far, just get the bottle."

Jill looked uncertainly at her. "Are you sure?"

"Yeah. This might be our only chance to..."

"To what?"

Katy didn't know, and with no answer forthcoming, Jill turned back to the shelf.

"What's happening?" said Katy.

Jill grunted.

"Can't... really... talk."

Katy heard the clink of teeth on glass, which made her shudder, followed by a scratching sound as the bottle scraped along the shelf. It was like a playlist of all her least favorite noises.

Jill turned to her, hunched over, the bottle dangling from her mouth. She looked ridiculous, and Katy had to choke back delirious laughter.

"Good," she managed to say. "Now bring it over."

Jill started to move, her feet shuffling laboriously across the floor. The bottle swung from her mouth like a pirate lantern, and Katy imagined a parrot resting on Jill's shoulder, squawking about—

Upstairs, a toilet flushed. A door closed again.

It was fine. Whoever had passed earlier would head back the way they came. She hoped.

Footsteps clumped along the hallway.

Jill tried to speed up, but with her ankles tied together, she had little success.

The footsteps stopped at the door. She heard the rattle of keys being fished out of a pocket.

"Oh god, hurry!" hissed Katy.

The keys jangled together.

Jill started to bunny hop her way towards the mattress. She wasn't even halfway back yet.

Katy fixed her eyes on the door.

"Don't drop the bottle," she said. "They'll hear you."

In the hallway, the keys clanged to the floor. The sound made Katy jump.

"Fuck," came a voice. It sounded like Corvo.

Katy's guts churned. She couldn't imagine what was going through Jill's head right now.

A rattle in the lock.

What to do? She hadn't expected this. In her head, everything had gone perfectly according to plan.

What plan?

"Too many fucking keys," muttered Corvo as he inserted another.

Katy looked at Jill. "You're nearly there," she said, tears stinging her eyes. Her friend needed help, and there was nothing — literally *nothing* — she could do.

Jill whimpered in response. It was true, she *was* over the halfway mark. She could still make it. If she—

Jill tripped.

It seemed to happen in slow motion.

She toppled forwards, the glass bottle clamped between her lips, hands behind her back, unable to prevent the fall, or the inevitable impact of the bottle shattering in her mouth.

Time slowed to a desolate crawl.

Jill bent her legs, trying to break the fall with her knees. She continued onwards, the stone floor rushing up towards her, towards the glass.

She closed her eyes and twisted her neck to the side.

The bottle struck the floor. It didn't shatter, just broke, like in the movies when the hero gets in a bar fight and smacks a beer bottle off the counter. There was another sound, the sickening thud of Jill's head hitting the floor, but it could have been worse.

Much worse.

At least she didn't have a bottle sticking out of the back of her head, or a mouthful of glass.

"You okay? Jill, you okay?"

Jill spat out the remains of the bottle neck and lay still, wheezing.

"I'm okay. I'm alright."

Another key rattled in the lock, galvanizing Jill. She slithered towards the mattress, forcing herself onto it.

"*Hey Bax,*" shouted Corvo. "*Where are the keys to the cellar? None of these fuckers work.*"

"*The big silver one,*" came Baxter's subdued response, and Katy closed her eyes, listening to Jill's gentle sobs as the door finally opened, letting a shaft of light in. A sixty-watt tungsten bulb had never felt so heavenly, casting its cheap celestial glow over the two girls lying on the mattress. Katy glanced over at the broken bottle. The ray of light wasn't wide enough to illuminate it. She breathed deeply.

That was too close.

Corvo stepped into the path of the light, hovering at the top of the stairs, holding a small tray. He came gingerly down the steps, the third one from the top groaning and bending under his weight. The tray wobbled, the two glasses tinkling together, clear liquid spilling over the sides.

Eventually, he arrived at the bottom, making his way towards them. They lay silent. It was too late to do anything about their blindfolds, which rested below their eyes. Corvo placed the tray on the ground. The oddly nostalgic aroma of chicken soup filled the air.

"I'm gonna untie you one at a time," said Corvo. "And then you can eat."

They didn't reply, and he turned Katy onto her front, struggling to undo her bindings. He left her legs tied. She sat, stretching her aching arms out, spreading her fingers wide, twirling her wrists.

Corvo held a bowl out to her. "There you go," he said.

She stared blankly at him. "There's no spoon," she said, her stomach grumbling noisily.

Corvo's posture slumped. "Just... eat it. Drink it. Whatever." He refused to make eye contact, looking instead at the wall.

Katy didn't want to argue. She raised the bowl to her mouth, her hands shaking from the surge of adrenaline, and drank. It was chicken noodle soup, the packet kind that her father favored. She thought of him, and a deep well of sadness filled within her.

Throw the hot soup in his face, then smash him with the bowl. Use the broken porcelain to cut through the remaining bonds and get out.

But she couldn't. Her bravado had deserted her. She told herself she didn't want to hurt anyone, and that of the four of them, Corvo seemed the... nicest?

He kidnapped you.

But he hadn't hurt her.

Yet.

The lukewarm soup tasted good. She swallowed the last of the noodles and offered the empty bowl to Corvo. He took it and handed her a glass of water. She greedily glugged it down.

"Give me your hands," he said.

"Wait a minute," she said softly. "Please. It hurts." She held up her hands, showing him the red marks where the rope had chafed her. "I won't run. I promise."

He looked at her for a long time.

"What could I even do?" she said. "You're so much bigger than me. So much stronger."

He glanced nervously back up the stairs.

"Fine," he said, "but keep them behind your back in case anyone sees."

It was too dark to say for certain, but she thought he was blushing.

"I will," she said. "Thank you."

"You try anything, and I'll rip you apart," he said, though he didn't sound like he meant it. He repeated the process for Jill while Katy stretched her arms out, enjoying the freedom of movement. As she did, she watched Corvo intently.

It was the first time she had seen his face, though the significance of this was apparently lost on him.

Every feature looked oversized, from his bulbous nose to his wide, witless eyes. He was a giant, well over six-feet-tall, with hands that could crush her skull with ease. Written on his t-shirt was the slogan RESTORE THE SKYWALKER SAGA from pit to sweat-stained pit. She had no idea what it meant.

"What are you gonna do with us?" she said. Corvo didn't respond. He gathered the bowls and glasses, balancing them on the tray. They kept sliding about.

He had clearly never worked in the service industry.

"Just keep quiet," he said. He turned to Jill. "Lie down on your front." She complied, lying still as he tied her wrists. "Now you," he said to Katy.

"I need to go to the bathroom," she said.

He shook his head. "Uh-uh, no way."

"Please, I've not been since this morning."

Corvo looked uncertain. "I, uh... I'll have to check with Bax."

"No! I'm about to pee myself. I need to go *now*."

He fidgeted, staring at his hands.

"I dunno..."

She turned on the tears again, sobbing exaggeratedly. It was a special skill she had honed over the years, especially useful for getting out of tidying her room, and it didn't take long for Corvo to break.

"Okay, *okay*. Jesus, fuck." He looked up at the door again. "But don't try anything dumb, or I swear…"

"I won't. Please, just help me."

"Fine. Follow me." The big idiot turned to head up the stairs. Katy rolled her eyes behind his back, then cranked the vulnerability up to eleven.

"You need to untie my legs. I can't move."

He stopped, sighing heavily. "Shit. I swear, if you run…"

"I know. You'll kill me."

He bent, his large hands struggling with the knots.

"I wouldn't do that," he said quietly. "We're not killers. We only want the money. You won't get hurt, not if you coordinate."

"You mean cooperate?"

"That's what I said."

"What about me?" said Jill quietly. Corvo looked surprised, as if he had forgotten she was there.

"One at a time," he said. Katy figured he wasn't used to dealing with girls. He seemed flustered, out of his element. The knot came loose, and her legs were free. She groaned with pleasure, working her numb ankles. Corvo took her under the arms and hoisted her into a standing position. Her knees buckled, and Corvo held her.

"What now?" he grumbled.

"I've not used my legs in a while," she said, adopting a girlish tone. "The ropes are too tight."

"Hurry up," he said, looking anywhere but at her.

She tested her weight and found she could stand.

"Okay," she said. Corvo led her up the stairs, gripping her arm with one big paw. She knew the toilet was to the left — it had flushed several times since their arrival — so was surprised when Corvo led her to the right. He saw her hesitate.

"Use the upstairs one. I don't want the others to see you."

So the building had two levels and a cellar. That was good to know.

Katy nodded, taking in the dubious sights of the hallway as Corvo accompanied her. Floral wallpaper in garish purples and yellows, a desk with a single dead flower in a vase, paintings of pastoral scenes in muted tones, each one featuring either a fish or a fisherman or a fishing boat.

"Fisherman's lodge?" asked Katy.

"How did you know?" said Corvo, sounding genuinely impressed.

"Women's intuition," she smiled.

He nodded, puzzled. They climbed a set of wooden stairs. The bathroom was behind the second door on the left. Corvo opened it like a gentleman.

"Be quick."

She stepped inside, closing the door. There was no lock.

Damn. Who doesn't put a lock on the bathroom door?

No worries. At least he hadn't come in with her.

The bathroom itself was disgusting. A filthy sink, the ceramic chipped and yellowing, above which hung a mirror encrusted with dirt. She could barely make out her own reflection, which was for the best. With what she had been through, she probably looked about thirty years old.

There was a bathtub in the corner, a shower curtain pulled halfway around. The tub was full of the filthiest liquid she had ever seen, dank and brown and sludgy, like something had *died* in there. A can of air freshener perched on the side of the tub.

"You nearly done?"

Katy had almost forgotten about Corvo.

"Not quite. I've... I've got my period."

She heard Corvo mutter, *"I don't need details,"* through the door.

She moved across the floor to the only window. It was small, very small, but she *might* be able to squeeze through. Not right now, though. Jill was still tied up downstairs.

Next time.

"Right, I'm coming in," said Corvo.

"Wait, I'm almost done."

She had almost forgotten she still had to pee.

When she was finished, she opened the door to find Corvo waiting, an agitated expression on his face. Without a word, he grabbed her arm and took her back down the stairs. Katy stole a quick glimpse down the hallway, but the doors were all closed.

No matter. There would be other times. What was it her teacher used to say? Ah yes.

Rome wasn't built in a day.

She could wait.

It was almost too easy.

9

———

Once Katy was alone, she wasted no time.

Corvo had grudgingly taken Jill upstairs to use the bathroom, but not before retying Katy's wrists and ankles.

When the door closed, plunging the cellar into darkness, the first thing she did was roll across the mattress to where Jill had fallen. She maneuvred her way carefully onto the floor and ran her hands along the ground, searching for the broken wine bottle. Her fingers nudged it and the bottle rolled away from her.

Damn! Take it slow.

But how could she? They would be back soon.

She located the neck of the bottle, twisting it around until the sharp edge faced the rope, and went to work. Corvo's knots were looser than the woman's. She sawed at the bindings, grimacing as the glass scratched back-and-forth across her skin.

The plan was falling into place. Soon, she would be free, and when Jill returned, Katy would untie her too. Then they would escape through the window, flag down a passing cop car, and be home in time for takeout.

Those dumb criminals would be left looking like fools. By the time they realized their captives had escaped, the FBI would have the place surrounded. She couldn't wait to watch the footage online.

The rope around her wrists came loose. She had done it!

A key in the lock.

She hadn't even noticed their footsteps. Katy rolled back onto the mattress, leaving the bottle on the floor. The door opened, Corvo and Jill descending the stairs. Once more, the third step from the top groaned under their weight.

Corvo retied Jill, picked up the tray, and went back up the stairs without another word. He locked the door behind him.

Katy turned to Jill, trying to suppress her excitement. "How you feeling?"

"How do you *think* I'm feeling?"

"I think you feel better now you've peed."

"Can't you take this even a little seriously?" said Jill, rolling over so her back was turned to Katy.

This is it. This is the moment.

Without warning, she jabbed her hand into Jill's side. The girl screamed.

"Hey, wait, it's me," laughed Katy. Jill turned to look at her through wide, frightened eyes, as Katy held her free hands in the air and wiggled her fingers. "See?"

Jill took several deep, dragging breaths before she was able to speak. When she managed to, it was not worth the wait.

"What... how..."

Katy grinned at her, unable to disguise her glee.

"While you were peeing, *I* was cutting through the ropes," she said, a little too smugly. She decided to reign in the attitude.

For now, anyway.

Once they were back home, Jill would never hear the end of it. Katy would tell everyone at school that she had freed them while Jill was peeing. She imagined Jill's red face as she tried to deny it, her every protestation making her seem even more guilty. She—

"What are you waiting for?" said Jill "Untie me!"

"Maybe I'll leave you here," Katy said playfully. "After all, you said I had a fat ass."

"You said I had a long neck!"

"I didn't say it was long," said Katy. "I just meant that if someone gave me a scarf that was ten sizes too big, I'd regift it to you."

"Katy, that's not funny. Hurry up before they come back." Jill sounded upset, but Katy couldn't help herself.

"Do I have a fat ass?"

"No. Now untie me."

"Which one of us has the fattest ass?"

"Jesus Christ, are you for real? We're in *danger,* Katy. What the *fuck.*"

Katy paused. Jill *never* swore. She was really pissed off.

"Jeez, way to overreact," said Katy.

Jill refused to look at her. "They'll *kill* us."

"They won't. How would they get their money? They need us alive."

"No, Katy," said Jill. "They need *you* alive." She took a deep breath and looked Katy in the eyes. "It doesn't matter what happens to me."

Katy had nothing to say to that.

It was true. Here she was, capering around, safe in the knowledge that they wouldn't hurt her... but had she considered Jill's feelings for even a second?

She hadn't. Shame seeped through her veins.

"I'm sorry," she said, her apology met with no acknowledgement. "I got carried away, that's all." She untied Jill's wrists and took one of her friend's hands. Jill pulled it away.

"I'm scared, Katy," she said quietly. She was crying again, her shoulders jerking up and down. "And I know you're treating it like a big joke, like everything else in your life. But this isn't one of your daydreams. This is our *lives* we're talking about, and... and..."

Katy tried to speak, but only a choked sob came out. Jill was right. She was *always* right.

"I'm sorry," she repeated, then she was crying too. She lay down next to Jill and put her arm around the girl's waist, holding her close. Jill rolled over to face her.

"I forgive you," she said, and sniffed loudly.

"You're my best friend," said Katy. "You know that, don't you?"

"I do."

"And your neck's not that long."

Jill smiled at Katy and said, "You still have a big fat ass, though."

Katy laughed. She leaned in and kissed Jill on the cheek.

"I love you," she said.

"Love you too, you loser." She pulled Katy into an embrace. Normally, Katy wasn't a hugger, but she felt she owed Jill this much.

"Wanna get out of here?" whispered Katy.

"You sure we can?"

"Positive. All we have to do is get those boards off the window."

"But what if we can't?"

Katy smiled. "How hard can it be?" She tried to pull free of the hug, but Jill clung on.

"Just one more minute," she said. "Please. It makes me feel like everything's gonna be okay."

Katy nodded. Why not? They had all the time in the world, and to be honest, she was enjoying the hug. All these years she had thought they were overrated, but it was actually quite pleasant. She decided to give her dad a hug when she got home. That would embarrass him!

"Okay," she said after a while. "You ready?"

Jill reluctantly released her. They untied their ankles and tottered arm in arm towards the boarded-up window, their legs tired and sore from lack of use.

The window was high, about six feet off the ground, but they could reach it if they stretched. Three planks had been nailed across, allowing only the thinnest sliver of moonlight through. Katy dragged a wooden fishing crate over and climbed on top. Her face was level with the window. Squinting through the gap, she could see the soft beauty of the ocean washing across the sand, bathed in the cool blue of night. The sight made her heart sing.

"Help me take these off," she said, squeezing her fingers under the planks. Jill clambered up alongside her. The wood was damp, rotten from the sea air, and it slid over the nails with little difficulty. The second plank proved just as simple, the soft timber crumbling in their hands. Katy smiled.

Too easy.

"Okay," she said, taking charge. "Once we're out, we stick together."

"We could steal their car," said Jill.

"Van," corrected Katy, needlessly. "And who's gonna drive it?"

Jill nodded. Neither of them could drive, so the van was out of the question. No, they would have to run, following the road until a car passed, or until they reached a town. Katy figured they'd have hours until the kidnappers noticed they were gone. They had just been fed, so she didn't believe they would return anytime soon. With any luck, no one would check on them until morning.

The last plank was tougher to remove.

It was newer, the wood less rotten. Katy and Jill took an end each, trying to wrench it free. The crate wobbled beneath them.

"It's not coming," said Jill. She looked at Katy, her face slick with perspiration. The plank remained in place. "What do we do?"

Katy sized up the window. The gap was narrow, but not impossible to fit through.

"We can make it," she said with all the conviction she could muster.

Jill gripped her arm. "Maybe we should just stay."

Katy shook her head. "There's no backing out now. We can't get the wood back over the window. If they find out we've tried to escape, then..." Katy smiled reassuringly. "Look, they won't be back for *hours*. By the time they check on us, we'll be talking to the cops." She held Jill's hand. "They won't even know we're missing."

She sensed the nerves emanating from Jill in waves. Her clammy hand trembled. Katy squeezed it, then reached into the gap and undid the window latch. She slowly lifted the pane. A tiny sand waterfall poured in through the widening gap. It was almost too perfect. There would be no distance to fall once they were through, thanks to the window being at ground height. Being trapped in a cellar had its advantages after all.

"Wanna go first?" asked Katy. Jill shook her head. "Okay, well help me up."

Jill cupped her hands, weaving her fingers together tightly. Katy put her foot on Jill's hands, readying herself.

"You got this, okay?" she said, then sprang up towards the window. She put too much effort in, going high and smacking her skull against the wooden board.

"You all right?" said Jill.

"Fine," she replied, though she wanted nothing more than to rub the top of her head, where a bump was surely already forming. Leaning forwards, she placed both hands on the side of the window frame and pulled herself through. The sea breeze swept across her skin, and she buried her face in the cool, inviting sand. Part of her wanted to stay here forever, just lying on the beach, but half her body was still dangling through a window, so she dug her hands into the sand and tried to claw her way out. When her ass reached the gap, she realized she could go no further. She wiggled and tried to flatten herself, but the gap was too narrow.

Jill was right!

Her confidence faltered. This wasn't part of the plan. In her dumb kidnap fantasies, she had slipped through the window like liquid, smooth and casual, not gotten her stupid ass stuck. It was kinda scary, and also embarrassing. Imagine they found her like this?

"Hey," she whispered. "I think I'm stuck."

"What?" said Jill, way too loud.

"Shhh! I said, I'm *stuck.* You need to give me a push."

"Okay," said Jill. She wrapped her arms around Katy's ankles and tried to lift her.

"No," said Katy. "It's my butt. You need to push it down."

"I need to what?"

"Just do it."

"I'm not pressing your butt down."

"You have to!"

There was a moment, followed by a grumpy harrumph, and then two hands squeezed down on Katy's ass. "I can't believe I'm doing this," she heard Jill mumble, and Katy burst out laughing. She couldn't help it.

"Are you laughing at me?" said Jill.

"No," giggled Katy. "It feels nice. We should do this more often."

"Right, that's it, I'm stopping."

"Wait til I tell everyone at school you couldn't keep your hands off my butt."

"You want me to leave you hanging there?"

Katy tried to control herself. They were wasting time, but the whole thing had turned into such an adventure that she was thoroughly enjoying herself now.

"Hurry up," she said. "Push me, or I'll fart on you."

"Don't you *dare!*"

"Then push. Come on, grab a handful."

"There's plenty to go around," said Jill.

"What did you say?"

"Nothing."

She felt Jill simultaneously pressing down on her ass and pushing forwards. Katy squirmed, her fingers unable to gain purchase in the sand.

"Are you clenching?" said Jill.

She was.

"It's helping. Almost... there," said Katy through gritted teeth. She realized Jill had stopped. "Hey. What's happening?"

There was a moment of silence.

"Oh god, Katy," said Jill. *"Someone's coming."*

Shit, thought Katy. *Shit, shit, shit.*

"They're probably going to the bathroom," she said, but her heart pounded unyieldingly. "Come on, push me."

She felt Jill's hands on her ass again, shoving her. There was a clump of dry grass within reach, and she grabbed it, wrapping it around her hand, pulling herself across the soft sand. Her butt squeezed through the window like a cork in a champagne bottle. She half-expected to hear an audible pop.

"I made it!" she said, hauling her legs through the remaining gap.

"I can hear the keys," said Jill, unable to hide the tremor in her voice. "They're opening the door."

Katy spun on the sand, holding her hands out for Jill to take. They shook wildly, and for the first time, she fully understood the gravity of the situation.

This was no game.

Should she return to the cellar? Would that be better? It was dark outside. They might never notice that the planks were gone from the window.

Too late.

Jill took her hands, gripped them, and tried to climb through.

"Oh my god, oh my god," she kept repeating.

Katy pulled. Her strength seemed to desert her. Jill had a tight hold on her, but Katy found herself sliding along the sand back towards the window. She shifted her body, planting both feet on either side of the frame.

"Come on," she said, closing her eyes, shutting out all sensory input save for the subtle lapping of the waves and the frantic rasping of Jill's shoes against the cellar wall.

"They're coming!" yelped Jill.

"Then *hurry.*"

She clutched Jill's hands, trying to yank her through. Jill looked over her shoulder. "Oh god," she said.

"I've got you," said Katy. She pulled with all her strength, and Jill's head appeared through the gap, her face streaked with tears. "See?" grunted Katy. "You're almost—"

A hand clamped over Jill's face, covering her nose and eyes. She opened her mouth to scream, but no sound came out. Instead, she choked a mouthful of blood onto the sand before jerking violently, the crimson liquid dribbling down her chin. A wet, ragged wheeze escaped her lips, and then Jill was gone.

"Jill?" Katy managed to say.

Varg's face appeared at the window, contorted with rage.

"You little cunt," he snarled. "I'll fucking kill you."

His hand shot through the open window, closing over her ankle, reeling her in like a fisherman with his catch of the day. Too frightened to scream, Katy realized all at once how badly she had misjudged the situation. There was something about Varg's expression that terrified her. His teeth gnashed like a feral dog, and Katy did the only thing she could think to do under the circumstances — she kicked him square in the nose with her free foot.

She had never heard a bone break before, but as her heel connected with the soft organ, she heard a brittle snap over Varg's startled, angry roar. His grip loosened, and she tried again, putting all her strength into the blow. This time his nose crushed under the impact. There was a dull thud as his body hit the cellar floor.

Katy lay flat across the sand, peering through the window, her heart hammering so hard that she struggled to breathe.

Jill was motionless on the floor, Varg alongside her, both of them seemingly out cold.

"Jill," she said. *"Jill!"*

A vast pool of blood surrounded her friend. Only then did Katy notice the enormous butcher knife next to Varg's open hand. It, too, was covered in blood.

Jill's blood.

She's dead, she's dead.

No! She was breathing. Katy was sure of it. Her chest rose incrementally, then fell. What the hell should she do? She couldn't leave Jill here. It would be a death sentence. On the other hand, she couldn't go back inside unless she walked round to the front door and rang the doorbell. Her mind was utterly, uselessly blank.

"Jill," she said again. She didn't know what else to do.

You killed her.

"No."

You did. Your stupid escape plan just got your best friend killed.

"It wasn't meant to be like this," she sobbed, tears streaming down her flushed cheeks. She had to decide, and decide fast. Jill might be dying, and Varg wouldn't be unconscious forever.

Run, screamed the voice in her head.

But what about Jill?

You're not running away, you're running for help. You need to get the cops.

"Yeah," she panted, her lower lip trembling. "The cops." She got to her feet, steadying herself against the exterior wall, a sickness rising in her stomach.

Get help. It's your only chance. It's Jill's only chance.

Willing herself to move, she broke into an unsteady jog, her boots sinking into the sand. She reached an embankment, climbed it, and ran. There was nothing to see. No lights, no buildings... nothing. Unending dunes of grassy sand wavered in the warm night breeze.

Pick a direction. Follow it. You're not on a desert island. There must be people nearby.

The tall grass was stiff and sharp, and slashed at her legs like thousands of paper cuts, but it was faster than running on the sand. Less tiring, too. Katy had never done well in gym class. She always finished second-last in track, and that was only because Greta Kirk was so slow that when she ran, she practically moved backwards. Hell, Katy had never been an academic over-achiever in *any* of her subjects, except for drama.

Is this what you're thinking about? School? Your best friend is dying!

"I know that," she sobbed breathlessly. "And I'm sorry."

She kept going. She couldn't stop now. Jill's life depended on her.

When she looked back at her progress, the building had vanished from sight. Rolling sand dunes surrounded her, spiky trees silhouetted against the navy sky like gnarled, evil creatures. She stopped a moment, listening, hearing nothing but the sinister howl of the wind, and tried to catch her breath. She thought of Jill, alone in that house, bleeding out, and started to run again.

She had to find someone.

She had to get help.

Jill heard Katy calling her name.

She wanted to respond, to call out, to leap to her feet and clamber out the window, but she couldn't move. Her limbs were blocks of ice. She could hear, she could see, and she could taste the coppery blood that coated her mouth, but that was it. From the neck down, she felt nothing. Not an itch, not a tingle. *Nothing.*

She was dying, and she knew it.

She hoped Katy could get to safety. Maybe, in an unlikely stroke of good fortune, she would find help, and they would arrive in time to save her.

Yeah. Sure.

It was a strange sensation, dying. In three weeks, Jill would have been seventeen. She had been asking for driving lessons for months, and figured that's what her parents had gotten her. They weren't rich like Katy's father, but they did okay, and spoiled Jill as best they could. She suddenly realized she would never see them again. What was the last thing they had said that morning as she left for school?

Have a good day, sweetheart.

And she had replied with, *Shut up, mom.*

She hadn't said it unkindly, but now Jill wished more than anything that she could go back in time and tell her mom she loved her. Her dad too, though he would be too wrapped up in the sports section to hear her, slurping his milk and spilling cornflakes down his shirt. He was such a messy eater. *We can't take you anywhere,* her mom would always say when they were at a restaurant and he inevitably spilled something down himself.

She knew she was crying, though she felt nothing. No delicate drops of water rolling down her cheek, no shiver running through her body.

"Fuuuuuuuuck," said someone next to her. She saw him in her peripheral vision. A thin, bald man with a graying beard. He turned to her, his lower face a mask of crimson gore, his nose twisted at a grotesque angle. He glanced at the window, then back to Jill. Indecision flickered across his face. Then he smiled, and Jill wished for something she had never wished for before.

She wished she were dead.

"Your friend won't get far, girly," he said, air whistling through the gap created by a missing tooth. He casually climbed on top of her, perching over her hips and looking intently into her eyes. "You can hear me, right?"

She blinked. It was all she was capable of.

"Yeah," he said, "I think you can. You broken, girly? You a cripple?" He rested his full weight on her, and she heard the wet squelch of her blood leaking through the wound in her back. "You gonna die on me, bitch?"

She wanted to scream at him, *shut up and get it over with! Shut up! Shut up!* But she could only blink. She could only fucking *blink*.

"I wish we had more time, girly, but you look like you're gonna die, and I ain't no corpse fucker." He reached for his knife and raised it. The serrated blade caught the moonlight and glinted, before plunging out of her line of vision. She heard it strike something hard, and for a second, she thought he had missed. Then a geyser of blood erupted from her stomach, hitting Varg in the face. The knife had gone right through her and struck the stone floor. He licked his lips, pulling the knife free, then rammed it back in with both hands, again, and again, and again, blood gushing over him.

"You fucking bitch," he said.

He wrenched the knife free from her stomach. Something pale and stringy was caught on the blade. He shook the weapon. Part of her long intestine slopped onto the cold stone floor.

Jill closed her eyes, listening as the blade penetrated her

flesh, ripping and tearing through skin and muscle, jerking her lifeless body.

After a while, even the sounds stopped, and she slipped quietly into nothingness.

10

—————

AT THE PRECISE MOMENT THAT JILL DREW HER FINAL BREATH, Baxter popped the cap on a beer and perched on a seat by the breakfast bar. He handed the bottle to Emma, ignoring Corvo, and retrieved one for himself.

"Cheers," he said, clinking his bottle against hers. She made no reply. Baxter scanned his eyes around the kitchen, trying to think of something interesting to say to break the awkward silence. Like the rest of the lodge, the kitchen was bedecked in fishing imagery. A black-and-white photo of a prune-faced old bastard holding up a fish that reached from the grass to his chest, its glassy, dead eye staring madly into oblivion. Three men in yellow rain slickers waving from a ship, their faces sullen, like smiling would be some ominous portent of doom. A watercolor illustration of an octopus capsizing a vessel, the crew members leaping in horror from the wreckage, landing in the sea where hungry sharks circled the blood-red water.

"Never figured you for an appreciator of art," said Emma.

"Huh?" said Baxter, caught by surprise.

She smiled mirthlessly. "Yeah, that's what I thought."

He was on the back-foot with her again. What was it about Emma that left him tongue-tied, unable to lead with his usual authority?

Probably the fact you want to fuck her.

"I like paintings," he blurted.

She just stared at him. "Oh yeah, I bet you're a real fucking connoisseur."

He didn't know what the word meant, so he half-smiled and took a drink. She was smarter than him, and that pissed him off. Well, she could throw around all the fancy words she wanted, but they were only here because of *his* plan. He was the brains. Not Emma, not Varg, and certainly not Corvo.

"I think it's going well," he said, changing the subject.

"You think it's going well?" she smirked. "So tell me. What are we gonna do with *two* of them?"

"We'll find out who the other girl is. More importantly, who her old man is. We might have doubled our investment."

"She's not worth shit. You see that cheap-ass jewelry around her neck?"

"Yeah, well," said Baxter. He hadn't noticed her jewelry. "Might get *something* for her."

"You're a moron," said Emma.

Without thinking, his hand slipped into his pants pocket, his fingertips brushing the switchblade. If anyone else spoke to him like that, he'd cut them. Anyone but Emma. God, he wanted to bend her over the breakfast bar and hate-fuck her.

"I ain't no moron," he said.

That's it? That's the best you got?

She looked at him like he was something she'd scraped off her shoe.

"Where's Varg?" she said.

"Dunno," he muttered, more concerned with whether he would rather screw her while she was wearing that wig or not. She seemed to notice he was looking at her hair, and pulled the wig off, dumping it on the floor.

"You got a thing for redheads?" she asked.

"I, uh…"

She laughed at him. Goddammit, the bitch just straight-up *laughed* at him. In the corner of the room, Corvo chuckled. Baxter whirled on him. "Something funny, asshole?" The switchblade was out now, reassuringly deadly in his hand, and pointed towards Corvo.

"No, boss," said the big man. Baxter nodded. It felt good to be in control again. Scoring points off Corvo was an easy sport, but always enjoyable.

"Go find Varg," said Baxter. "Make sure he's not fucking around with the girls. That's the last thing we need."

"Yeah, okay," said Corvo. He remained seated.

Baxter waited. "Now, you dumb fuck."

"Oh, sure," said Corvo, standing and brushing crumbs off his shirt. He left the room, leaving Baxter and Emma alone. The thought made Baxter unaccountably nervous.

"That guy, huh?" he said.

"Yeah," said Emma coldly. "That guy."

"Yeah."

Jesus, say something smart.

But it was too late for that.

"I'm going to bed," said Emma.

"What's the time?"

"Who cares?"

He nodded as she picked the wig up off the floor. It hung from her hand like a scalp.

"Goodnight," he said, and she glared at him. Keen to stop her leaving, he said, "We'll call Ketcher at noon."

She turned to him. For the first time that evening, Emma looked interested in something he had to say. "You sure he'll pay?"

Baxter took a long drink. "He already lost his wife. To get his daughter back, he'd cut his own goddam balls off."

"I don't want his balls," she said with the trace of a smile. "I want his money."

Baxter stood, tucking the switchblade back into his pocket. "And I'm gonna get it for you."

"You do that," she said quietly.

He took a tentative step closer to her. "Twenty million's a lot of money."

She licked her lips. "I know."

"It can buy you anything you want."

She glanced down between his legs. "I know what *you* want."

"You have no idea," he said. He moved towards her. He could smell her perfume, the scent intoxicating. It reminded him of those early fumbles in the bedrooms of teenage girl-friends, terrified their parents would walk in and find him balls-deep in their daughter.

His hands found Emma's waist, sliding down to her ass.

She leaned in close and whispered in his ear.

"Get your fucking hands off me, you—"

The kitchen door burst open.

Emma shoved Baxter away from her as Corvo — red-faced and breathless — entered the room.

"It's Varg," he said.

Baxter shared the briefest of glances with Emma, then

pushed past them both, heading into the hallway. The lights were off. He fumbled in his pocket for his phone as something shambled out of the darkness towards him.

Varg.

He was covered in blood. The dark fluid coated his face and chest, dripping down his torso like wet paint.

"What the fuck have you done?" said Baxter, his whole body vibrating with crazed, psychotic anger.

Varg smiled, baring a row of red teeth.

"I must have slipped," he said, and started to laugh.

Katy could no longer hear the waves.

The loose grains of sand had given way to denser ground the further she got from shore. She had avoided the road, heading for an area of thick woodland ahead. They would come for her, and when they did, they would take the van. How long did she have? The lights of the cabin had faded from view, yet she had seen nothing, heard nothing. What was taking them so long? Or had they passed her already? No, that was impossible. She would have heard the engine in the eerie calm, would have seen the headlights weaving their way drunkenly through the night as they searched for her.

Should have taken your phone from the van.

Dammit, why did she only think of that now? But she knew why. Because she had been *scared*. She thought she had no time.

Her legs screamed in protest. No longer able to run, she slowed to a jog, and by the time she reached the trees, dawn was breaking, golden light splintering through the branches. Had she truly run all night? And if so, why hadn't she seen anyone yet?

She came to a stop, placing her hands on her knees and leaning forwards, panting. Her heart pounded ceaselessly in her chest. She must have *killed* Varg. It was the only explanation. The way his head had smacked off the cellar floor... it was possible. It was all too possible.

She tried to catch her breath.

Jill's dead.

No, she didn't *know* that. She could still be—

She's dead, and you killed her.

Katy started to cry. She stumbled onwards, exhausted. The hazy sun hovered above the horizon, and she wondered how far she had come. She regretted not following the beach along the coast. They would not have expected her to do that, and chances are she would have come across another lodge sooner or later. Anything but the endless emptiness that surrounded her like a post-apocalyptic wilderness. As she reached the line of trees, something caught her eye.

Movement.

It was nothing, the glint of the sun on a puddle, or in the eye of a hungry coyote, or—

It was a car. The vehicle shimmered in the heat like a half-remembered dream. She could hear it now, the casual fury of its engine, the brittle crunch of gravel beneath the tires. She spotted the track, not far away, and raised her arms, wanting to call out but unable to, her throat tight and raw. The car kept coming. There was no way the driver wouldn't see a bedraggled schoolgirl in the middle the road. She collapsed to her knees, praying the driver would stop and not just take a wide berth around her. Surely life couldn't be that cruel?

Tell that to Jill.

The vehicle was coming straight for her. She raised her hands, but the gesture was half-hearted. She was so tired, so out of breath.

This is it, then, she thought.

The brakes screeched, the car coming to an abrupt stop, the fender inches from her face. A wave of dust clouded over her. She choked a little and closed her eyes. They were wet, and she let the moisture drip down her cheeks to her cracked lips. A door opened, two feet stepping firmly onto the track.

"Help," she croaked, waving one hand, knowing how feeble she must look. The driver walked steadily towards her. She waved away the dust, squinting her eyes as the shadowy figure approached. She realized she should have been more cautious.

"No," she whispered.

It's not the van. Everything will be okay.

But surely they have another vehicle?

Footsteps crunched towards her, the dust stinging her eyes, the sun rising behind the man, turning him into a hulking black silhouette.

"Please," she whispered.

The man stood before her, blocking the sun.

He placed a hand on her shoulder.

"My god, sweetheart, are you all right?" he said.

The dust cleared, revealing an old face, lined with wrinkles.

The man crouched before her, pushed up the brim of his Lakers baseball cap, and gave her a worried look.

"Help me," was all she could say.

11

———

SHE DREAMED OF BEING BACK HOME.

Katy Ketcher had never been one for exciting, psychedelic dreams. She secretly envied those who would come to class and regale their friends with tales of the wild nightmare they had that night, though sometimes she thought they were making it up for attention. Her own dreams were always grippingly banal. Often, she would imagine that a parcel she had been waiting for arrived, or that she had gone for a walk and seen a nice tree. Nothing shocking, nothing thrilling. In this dream, she had been lounging on her bed in her pajamas, watching *Queer Eye*. The episode was a sad one, and she cried as Karamo gave one of his inspiring speeches.

She was still crying when she awoke in the passenger seat of the car. At first, she didn't move. Glancing furtively out the window, she could see the ocean, the cloudless sky turning it a deep shade of cerulean blue before it vanished behind a line of trees.

"You awake?" asked the man, his voice as soothing as a warm bath. He sat hunched over in the driver's seat, eyes narrowed, both hands on the wheel. He was even older than she had first thought. Beneath his baseball cap was thick white hair. His skin was loose across his skull, sagging at his chin. He turned to her. "Don't worry, you're safe now," he said.

She nodded. Hot sun streamed in through the windshield, battling with the pleasing coolness of the air con. She tried to speak, but no words came. The man slowed the car while he rummaged in the glove compartment.

Katy's heart stopped.

He's got a gun. He's one of them.

She flinched as he pulled out a water bottle and handed it to her.

"Here, drink this."

It's poison.

No, that was stupid. Who used poison anymore? This wasn't a fairy tale. She unscrewed the cap and glugged the liquid down.

The man chuckled. "Don't gulp it. Just small sips, or you'll make yourself sick."

She looked at him, at his pleasant, concerned face, and did as instructed.

"You been out all night?" he asked.

She tested her voice, producing a foul croak. She took another drink, sloshing the liquid around her mouth. It hurt to swallow.

"The cops," she said. "Call the cops. My friend is hurt."

"Take it easy and tell me all about it."

"There's no time. You have a phone?"

The old man looked embarrassed. "Not on me. Don't really understand those fancy cellulars the kids have these days. There's one at my cabin, though. That's where we're headed. Now why don't you tell me what happened? You here with your parents? You lost?"

"They kidnapped me. My friend too."

He looked away from the road, stared right at her. "Who did?"

"I don't know. Four of them. They took me and Jill, put us in a van, tied us up. I escaped, but they got Jill. I think they stabbed her. Please, you have to call the cops."

"Lord in heaven, are you serious? Why would they want a little thing like you? You got a rich daddy, or something?"

"Something," she said, suddenly wary of revealing too much and giving him ideas.

"They hurt you?"

"Just a little." She leaned against the window, the car juddering over uneven terrain.

"Well, it's not far to my cabin. A few miles. It ain't much, but there's a phone and a first aid kit. Where's your friend?"

She realized she didn't know. "I think some sort of fishing lodge by the sea."

"Gerry's place," said the man grimly. "Funny, I thought I'd seen someone over there the other day. Gerry's been dead two years, but sometimes his kids spend the weekend there. Figured it was them. Guess my old eyes don't work so well anymore. Probably shouldn't even be driving. You're lucky I didn't run right over you back there." He smiled at her. "The name's Pete, by the way."

He offered his hand, and she shook it. His grip was slack, and she swore she could feel the bones rattling around inside the skin.

"Katy Ketcher," she said quietly, her throat still sore. "Pleased to meet you."

"Katy Ketcher, well ain't that a sweet name. Happy to make your acquaintance, Miss—"

The car jolted forwards, snapping Katy's head back into the seat. Pete almost lost control of the vehicle, spinning the steering wheel at the last second before they rolled into the dunes.

"What the devil?" said the old man as he struggled to maintain control. Katy pivoted in her seat and looked through the rear windshield, knowing full well what she'd find there.

The white van, bearing down on them. It moved closer, ramming them again, and Katy instinctively reached for her seatbelt, clicking it in.

"It's them!" she said. "Drive faster!"

The car juddered, the tires sliding across the track and sending waves of stones hurtling through the air, rattling against the front of the van like machine gun fire.

"They're trying to run us off the road," grunted the man. Had he only just realized? The wheel spun out of his hand as the van struck them once more, and Katy reached over, grabbing it, holding it steady.

"*Go faster!*" she shouted.

Pete's foot pressed down on the accelerator. Katy looked back and saw Baxter behind the wheel of the van, Emma next to him, their faces set and hard as the van came at them again. Through the rear window it looked like a special effect in a 3D movie.

"Come on," she pleaded. The old man was rattled, his eyes wide and confused. Surely this car could outrun a massive white van?

"Why?" Pete kept asking.

Money, she wanted to say, but this was not the time. Trees shot by outside, the wheels of the car bouncing wildly across the ground. They took a corner too fast, too wide. The back tires skidded, turning the car ninety degrees.

The van was coming straight for them. She heard the high-pitched shriek of the brakes — *can't damage the merchandise, right?* — but it was too late. The white vehicle smashed into the side of Pete's car, plowing into the driver's side. The door buckled and bent, crushing the old man's legs and showering him in broken glass.

For a moment, nothing happened. Then Pete's head slowly pivoted towards her.

"Get out," he said, between long, irregular breaths.

She unclipped her belt, reached for the door, and hesitated. Pete stared forwards, blood spilling from his mouth.

"Go!" he cried, and she did. She flung the door open and scrambled out, straight into the waiting arms of Emma. The woman grabbed her, and Katy — with nothing left to lose — head-butted her. Her forehead caught the woman's cheek. Emma roared in pain and staggered backwards. Katy spun on her heels, ready to run.

Baxter was right there.

He lunged for her, gripping her forearms. She kicked him hard in the shin. The man flinched but didn't let go, spinning her and wrapping his arms around her stomach in an unshakable bearhug. She tried to squirm free, but her strength had abandoned her.

"Look what she did," snarled Emma, pointing to her cheek. It was already starting to discolor.

"You still look good," said Baxter hesitantly.

"Fuck off," she said, turning her attention to the wrecked car. She broke into a smile. "Hey," she said. "Check him out."

Katy followed the woman's gaze. Pete lay across the passenger seat. In his hand he clutched a pistol. He kept trying to raise it, to point it at Baxter, but every time his hand dropped back to the seat. He looked as spent as Katy felt.

"Let her go," he wheezed. He coughed up a mouthful of blood, his dentures dropping from his mouth and landing on the dirt.

"Oh my god," laughed Emma. "His fucking teeth fell out."

Emma strode towards him and crouched by his side. He peered up at her like a wounded animal, and Katy thought her heart might burst.

"Leave him alone," she said.

Emma knocked the baseball cap off the old man's head and ran a hand through his hair. "You trying to be a hero, pops?" she said. She plucked the gun from his hand. "Here, let me help you."

Pete opened his mouth. More blood dribbled out. Emma placed the barrel against the old man's cheek. She turned to Katy, smiled, and nonchalantly pulled the trigger. There was a deafening report as the bullet ripped through Pete's skin, thundering through his open mouth and bursting forth from his other cheek. It planted itself in the chassis with a shrill metallic clang.

Pete's head wobbled, blood pouring down his chin.

The woman fired again.

Katy screamed, closing her eyes, knowing full well she'd never be able to unsee this. She heard the wet splatter of blood gushing onto the ground. When she opened her eyes, Pete was staring at her, his head lolling to the side.

"You done?" said Baxter, his grip on Katy never lessening.

Emma sighed contentedly and pocketed the weapon. "Yeah," she breathed. "That felt good."

"You killed him," sobbed Katy.

Baxter's hold on her reflexively tightened as Emma came towards her. She traced a soft finger down Katy's face.

"If you'd stayed put, he'd still be alive," she said, then waved a dismissive hand, signaling the end of the conversation. She stared at Baxter. "I thought you said we were alone out here."

"I said we were seven miles from anyone," said Baxter, his voice loud in Katy's ear. "Guess this old fart was our neighbor."

Emma surveyed the damaged car. "Think anyone will find him?"

"Not anytime soon."

"Based on what?"

He didn't answer.

"Let's get out of here," he said instead. "We've got a call to make."

12

They had left Jill's body untouched.

When Baxter opened the cellar door, the cloying, sickly sweet odor of blood seeped insidiously into Katy's nostrils. She gagged. He led her down the stairs to the mattress, where he rebound her wrists and ankles. As she lay still, Baxter and Emma swept up the broken glass and studiously removed every item they could carry from the dingy room. Corvo was enlisted to board up the window again.

This time, they were taking no chances.

Katy lay on the mattress, staring at her friend's corpse. She wasn't just dead... she had been mutilated. Destroyed. Her face was no longer recognizable, a wet, red patchwork of scars and wounds, flaps of loose skin sagging from her skull. She had been split open from navel to chest, her white school shirt now a deep, putrid crimson.

Katy tried to make sense of it. That was Jill, her best friend, lying there. But it was impossible to reconcile the disemboweled horror with the smiling face and sweet nature of Jill. It was Saturday, and they should have been going to the movies today, most likely followed by a Five

Guys (a bacon cheeseburger each, large fries to share) and a stroll through the mall.

Never again.

Once the cellar had been emptied, Baxter ordered the others upstairs. He perched on the mattress and waited until he and Katy were alone, passing the switchblade from one hand to the other.

Katy watched the weapon move like the ticking hands of a clock. He wouldn't kill her, she was sure of that. But he could hurt her. He could hurt her badly.

"See what happens when you try to escape?" he said calmly, pressing the sharpened point of the blade into the tough flesh of his thumb. He gestured over to Jill without looking. "See what you did?"

"Please," said Katy, "I didn't—"

Baxter was on her in a flash. He grabbed her hair, yanking her neck, and dragged her towards Jill, her bare knees scraping over the floor.

"Do you see what you did?" he roared. *"Do you fucking see?"*

She stared into Jill's vacant eyes, two white orbs set into a sunken mass of bloodied meat.

"Stop!" sobbed Katy. She tried to push away, to turn her head.

"You did this!" said Baxter. "It's all your fault!"

He tugged hard on her hair, positioning her face above Jill's open torso.

Katy gagged. She could see *inside* her friend. Up close, the stench was unbearable.

"I'm sorry!" she cried. She couldn't take much more.

"You're sorry? You're fucking sorry? Tell that to her!" screamed Baxter, and then he thrust her face-first into her friend's stomach. The slippery organs were cold and wet against her skin, her cheeks, her lips. She closed her mouth, but it was too late. Something soft brushed her tongue.

"Do you see what you did you little cunt?"

She fought, desperate and horrified, but he held her there, pressed into the belly of her best friend, until he wrenched her out by her hair, a clump of it tearing off in his fingers. She fell, gasping, onto her side. Her guts churned, and she vomited while Baxter sat and watched, slowly rotating the switchblade like some amateur magician. When she was finished, he hoisted her beneath her arms, dumping her on the mattress. She wept, unable to look at him, the taste of blood — and worse — coating the inside of her mouth.

"I'm a reasonable man," said Baxter. "Believe me, I wanted nothing more than for this to go off without a hitch. We snatch you, we get the money, we give you back. It's simple, really. Your friend? That was unfortunate, but I can adapt. I've always been able to. So we had an extra body... so what? It becomes a package deal. Maybe her daddy's rich too, or maybe not. It doesn't matter. We got you, and that's what counts." He sighed, loud enough to let her know his disappointment. "Then you go and pull a stupid stunt like that, and your friend ends up dead. I bet you blame us for that, huh?"

She forced herself to look at him. "He killed her," she said.

Baxter shrugged. "Varg's an animal. He's like a cornered dog, but that's just how he lives his life. It's how he survives. I wouldn't have let him hurt either of you, not if you'd done what you were told and been good little girls. Oh, he would have tried, for sure, but I would have stopped him." He edged closer, brushing her vomit-flecked hair from her face. "Your friend's dead, but *you* still have a chance. I'm gonna call your daddy today, and arrange a deal. Once he pays, you go free." His fingers closed around her hair again, pulling taut, stretching her head back. The switchblade sprang open, the blade nudging her exposed jugular.

"Just don't try that again, okay?" he said.

She nodded as best she could. "I won't."

Satisfied, he withdrew the blade and stood, looking down at her with contempt. "I'll get Corvo to bring you some water so you can clean yourself up. You look fucking disgusting."

He started up the stairs, then turned back one more time.

"Don't you *ever* try that again," he said, and then the cellar door slammed shut and Katy was alone.

13

The clock struck twelve.

It was shaped like a fish. A salmon, Baxter thought, though he couldn't be sure. He hadn't been fishing since he was a child. What he did recall — in graphic, frightening detail — was the vision of his father reeling in a trout, the creature flapping helplessly on the line, a hook embedded in its mouth.

"Get a rock," his father had said, and young Baxter — no more than eight or nine years old — had picked up a fist-sized stone. It felt weighty in his hand, powerful, and when his father had lain the fish down on the embankment and said the word, Baxter had clubbed it over the head.

"We're just putting it out its misery," said his father, yet when Baxter stopped, he could see he had knocked one eyeball out of its socket. His father had looked at him proudly that day, and said, *"We'll make a man of you yet, son."*

"You gonna make the call?"

That was Emma. She rested her chin on her hands, staring at him with her usual bored expression. Baxter wondered if anything other than money excited her.

You saw the way she shot that old man. She seemed to get off on that too.

Okay, so money and killing. That was fine. He could supply her with money soon, no problem. And killing? Well, he may be able to arrange that too. He hadn't planned on killing the Ketcher girl, but the way things were going, it was fast becoming an inevitability.

Corvo perched on the breakfast bar, guzzling a sandwich. He squeezed it in his big sausage fingers, the mayonnaise dribbling from between the slices of bread and down his hand. The image disgusted Baxter, so he turned to Varg instead. It was no better.

"You gonna take a shower?" asked Baxter.

Varg regarded him calmly, his face coated in dried, cracked blood. It was in his pores, his hair, his teeth, beneath his fingernails. His clothes were covered in it. He looked at Baxter and shrugged.

"Maybe later."

Baxter knew better than to argue with a psychopath. Varg and Corvo had been cellmates at some point, a hideous friendship forged through unfortunate circumstances. Baxter didn't know what either of them had been in for, and it wasn't his place to ask. Perhaps Emma knew? After all, it was she who had suggested Corvo for their little heist. *A bit of muscle,* she had said, glancing disdainfully at Baxter's slender frame. They had been in a bar at the time, Baxter laying out his initial plans for the kidnapping, and she—

"The call?" said Emma in a harsh voice that could kill an erection at twenty paces.

"Yeah, I'm gonna," he said, annoyed at the hint of petulance in his voice.

Corvo giggled, and Baxter shot him a look.

"Sorry," said the big man, his mouth full of sandwich. "I'm nervous."

Jesus. One of the crew is a psychotic degenerate, the other a muscular coward.

"Alright," said Baxter, "Let's do this. Time to see how much Mr. Big Shot Hollywood Producer loves his daughter."

Emma laughed an empty laugh. "Real tough guy," she muttered.

He hated the way she undermined him in front of the others, and pretended not to hear. A burner phone sat on the table, a solitary number stored on the contacts. Butterflies danced in his stomach as he hit the button and waited for someone to answer. This was it. His ticket to the big time. He looked at Emma, smiled at her. She didn't smile back.

A female voice crackled out. *"Good afternoon, Paramount Studios publicity department, how may I help you today?"*

"Hello, yeah, I... *shit.*"

He hung up and slammed his fist off the table.

Emma stared at him in disbelief. "Hello? Who are you, Mr. Polite? Hello? You're a fucking criminal mastermind, you dumb shit. You don't start by saying fucking *hello.*"

"I know! I fucking know. Jesus, I forgot." Color flushed his cheeks, burning them, and the more he tried to calm himself, the worse it got.

"Real slick, Bax," said Varg through his bloody facemask. The dried fluid had taken on a dark-brown hue.

"Fuck you," said Baxter.

He grabbed the phone, dialed again, and waited. A different woman answered.

"Good afternoon, Paramount Studios publicity department, how may I help you today?"

Baxter cleared his throat, dropping his voice an octave. "I need to speak to Kevin Ketcher."

"I'm sorry, sir, you've reached the publicity department. If you're looking to speak to Mr. Ketcher, you'll have to contact him through his agent or personal publicist." She spoke with the bubbly voice of a co-ed.

"I *need* to speak to him." He paused for dramatic effect, then growled, "I have his daughter."

"I'm very sorry, but Mr. Ketcher is not here. This is the publicity department. I don't have a direct line to Mr. Ketcher, and I imagine he's a very busy man. If you have a script you'd like him to read, you may contact him through his agent or personal publicist."

"I don't think you understand," he said, trying not to show his frustration. "I have to speak with him urgently."

"Sir, I've already told you, this is the publicity—"

"I don't care if you're the goddam *sanitation* department, I want to speak to Kevin Ketcher *right now!*"

A pause. He had done it, he had gotten through to this motherfucking airhead bimbo on the—

"Sir, I'm afraid I'm going to have to ask you to watch your tone, or I will have no choice but to terminate the call and report you to the authorities for threatening behavior."

Not the police, shit!

"Okay, I'm..." he felt all eyes on him, judging him, mocking him. "...I'm sorry I yelled. But you have to get Kevin Ketcher on the phone." He lowered his voice again. "I have his daughter."

That's it, you're back on track. Nice and sinister!

"I see, sir." Another pause. *"Are you her babysitter?"*

Varg laughed out loud, cracks forming in his bloody face, splitting from the corners of his eyes like he was rapidly ageing.

"No, I'm not the fu—"

He caught himself in time.

"I'm not her babysitter. I've kidnapped her, and if you don't get Kevin Ketcher on the phone *right this second,* I'm going to kill her."

"If this is a publicity stunt, sir, I think it's in very poor taste. And might I remind you, we do not accept unsolicited scripts through the publicity department."

"This is no *stunt,*" he said, spitting out the last word like poison. "This is real!"

"Sir, if this was real, why would you be calling the publicity department?"

It was a good question. A *damn* good question. The whole debacle was spiraling out of control. He felt his blood pressure rising.

"Look, I'm a serious man, and I mean business. Get me Kevin Ketcher on the phone, now!"

"Sir, I'm going to have to ask you once more to watch your tone."

"I've kidnapped his daughter!"

Another pause. *"Sir, we don't accept unsolicited scripts through the publicity department."*

"It's not a script! It's..." He felt he might explode. "I *have* her. I..." He sighed. "Do you have his agent's number?"

"I'm sorry, sir, I can't give out that information. Is there anything—"

He jabbed the button and cut her off, then sat staring at the phone. "No one say a fucking word, or else—"

Varg burst out laughing. It was all the excuse Baxter needed. He got to his feet, charging at Varg. Corvo leaped from the breakfast bar, throwing himself between the two men.

"Enough!" shouted Emma.

Baxter turned to her, grateful for the interruption. She

held the old man's gun in her hand, pointing it in their general direction. She thumbed the safety.

"Quit pointing that gun at me," said Baxter.

She didn't. "Quit acting like a fool. Make the call."

"You heard the bitch on the phone. I don't have the number."

"So *get* the number."

"Sure, I'll just pull it out of my ass, huh?"

Emma's eyes narrowed to slits. "I thought you said you *had* his phone number."

Baxter took a deep breath. "I said I had *a* phone number."

"For the publicity department."

"That's right." He averted his eyes. "I, uh, got it from the internet."

Emma nodded. "I thought you were the brains of the operation?"

Varg snickered, and Baxter turned to him again.

"You got something to say?" he challenged.

He knew fighting Varg was a bad idea — the man was a fucking maniac — but for this ransom to work, he had to maintain authority.

"I have an idea," said Corvo.

It was the break Baxter needed. He grinned, taking a step back. "Oh, wait everyone, Corvo has an idea. Let's all stop and listen to Corvo's *big idea.*" He chuckled. "This oughta be good."

Corvo shrugged. "You want the guy's number, right?"

"Glad you're keeping up," said Baxter. Varg laughed, the tension in the room dissipating.

Corvo looked down to his feet. "I just mean... his daughter's downstairs. Why don't we ask her?"

A prolonged period of silence followed.

"Huh," said Baxter. "That's not a bad idea."

Corvo smiled guilelessly. "You mean that?"

"Yeah. I was, uh, just thinking the same thing," lied Baxter.

"Why not get *her* to do the talking?" said Emma. "Then they won't be able to identify our voices."

"Can they do that?" asked Baxter.

"Probably."

"Shit. Okay. Corvo, go and get the little bitch." He ran a hand through his hair. "Let's get this over with."

14

———

The smell was getting worse.

It had gone from a pungent sweet odor to a foul stench like the outdoor toilets at a festival. Now it was akin to raw meat on a hot summer's day. Flies buzzed around Jill's body. Katy imagined there were maggots there too, feasting on the decaying flesh of her friend. Somehow, she could *feel* the smell on her skin. How long would they keep them both down here? Surely at some point they'd have to... *dispose* of Jill.

Or you.

She shivered. She had seen their faces now. All of them. Four kidnappers, two of them murderers, and she could identify each one by face and name.

Things were not looking good.

They would kill her. There was no doubt in her mind. She would serve her sad little purpose, and then they would slaughter her like they had Jill. Sixteen years old, and her life was over. Her chance to escape had passed, as fleeting as a shooting star lighting up the night sky.

So what now? You gonna lie here and wait to die?

She looked at the steps that led up to the door. There were thirteen of them. She knew this, because she had counted them over and over. When you're trussed up in a murder-cellar, you gotta make your own entertainment.

Thirteen steps, but there may as well have been a thousand. Even if she could somehow stand and make her way up, the door was locked. She needed the key. Which of the kidnappers kept it? Probably Baxter. Unless they all had a copy? Varg had come in last night as they tried to flee. She didn't want to think about why he was coming to see them by himself.

What are you doing? You've already tried and failed to get out. Consider it a lesson learned. Play along with them, do what they say, and you still stand a chance.

It was sage advice. But this was no longer about escaping. This was about—

What?

She wasn't sure.

Revenge?

Maybe. As crazy as it sounded, yeah, why not? Revenge. They had butchered Jill. They deserved it.

They'll kill you.

So? She was going to die here. There was no sense in believing otherwise. A murder witness could not be allowed to live. And when you've nothing left to lose, and your back's against the wall...

Don't be an idiot.

Too late for that.

So what are you going to do, huh? You're tied up, alone.

Okay, so there was no way to free herself. She would have to get someone else to do it for her. But who?

A key fidgeted in the lock. She waited — for what else could she do? — as the door opened and a dark figure stood silhouetted against the hallway light. Corvo. She could tell by his size. He came down the stairs slowly.

"Hey," he said. "Bax wants to see you." He sounded apologetic, and it infuriated her.

"Couldn't he come visit himself?"

Corvo kneeled by the mattress. "I'm sorry about your friend. It wasn't supposed to be like this. It's just Varg, you know. He's got a temper."

"He gutted her," she said, the words foreign and absurd to her ears.

"You shouldn't have tried to run."

"What would *you* do if someone kidnapped you?"

He looked blank, as if he had never considered how she must feel. "No one would want me," he said. "And you're so rich."

"My dad is, yeah. He worked for it. And because of that, you're gonna kill me?" she said, unwilling to soften the edge in her voice.

"No," he said, shocked. "No one's gonna kill you. Bax says we won't."

"I don't care what he says. Jill's dead, and I'm next."

"I won't let it happen," he said, sounding small. "I promise."

"It's too late for promises."

He had no answer to that. He began to untie her legs, his fingers struggling with Baxter's knot.

"There's still time to change things," said Katy.

"There's no time."

"You could be a hero."

He shrugged almost imperceptibly. "Heroes don't look like me."

He was right, but she didn't say so. "Just let me go. I won't tell anyone. It'll be our little secret."

"Shut up," he said. The knot came loose. "If I did that, they'd kill me for sure."

She stretched her throbbing legs, her ankles red and burned from the bindings. He started to work on her wrists.

"Please," she said. She didn't feel like crying — she was too angry — but she forced the tears out, turning to look at him with her big, wet puppy-dog eyes. She knew the instantly disarming effect they had on her father. Corvo, however, refused to meet her gaze.

"I can't," he said. "But no one's gonna hurt you. I'll make sure of it."

She hadn't believed him the first time he'd said it, and still didn't.

"I would've gone and got her," said Varg, lighting up a cigarette.

Baxter fixed him with a stare. No matter what, it was imperative he kept Varg under control.

"You already killed one of them."

You fucking maniac, he almost added.

"She was trying to escape. Didn't have no choice."

"You couldn't just overpower a little girl? You had to fucking slice her open?"

"She wasn't worth nothing anyway."

"We don't know that."

"Whatever, man. We're supposed to be criminals, and you're all, *don't rape anyone, don't kill anyone.*" He took a long draw of his smoke. "This is turning into a real drag."

Baxter looked at Emma. She smirked. Why did nothing faze her? Things were not going according to plan, and she sat there smiling like the whole thing was a joke.

"He's got a point," she said.

"I do?" said Varg.

She nodded. "There are two dead already. I think the 'no murder' rule is out the window."

Baxter exhaled, trying to stay calm. "You know what looks worse than two murders on a rap sheet? *Three fucking murders.*"

"What do you care?" asked Emma, her manner accusatory. "Your hands are clean."

"I could kill if I wanted to," he said.

"Sure," she said. "But you're better than that, right? You're too smart, with your *plan.*"

He rubbed the bridge of his nose. "That's right. We're in this for the money, remember?"

"So what are you gonna do with her once we *get* the money? She's seen all our damn faces now."

She was testing him. His leadership was at stake. He had already fucked up the phone call, then lost his cool with Varg. Now this. A motherfucking *power struggle.* What he said next would be important. He had to earn their respect.

"Once we get the money," he said, "we can do whatever we want."

"So we kill her?" said Emma.

"Sure." He smiled for their benefit. "Why not?"

"I want her first," said Varg. "I'm gonna—"

A noise from the doorway.

Corvo, clearing his throat. Beside him stood Katy Ketcher, her face phantom-pale. Had she heard?

It doesn't matter, thought Baxter.

In twenty-four hours, she would be dead, and he — preferably with Emma by his side, or in his bed — would be far, far away.

15

———

KATY HELD THE PHONE, LOOKING AT IT THE WAY AN ALIEN would regard unfamiliar technology. It was black and chunky, with a tiny green screen. Much of it was taken up by buttons, and a small antenna protruded from the top. Katy had seen these types of phones in memes, but never actually held one.

"Call your dad," said Baxter.

Katy placed the phone down on the table with a loud *thunk*. God, it was so heavy!

"I need my phone," she said.

"Uh-uh," said Baxter, shaking his head. "You've got a perfectly good phone right there, and you can't Facebook someone when we're not looking." He put his hand on the burner phone and slid it towards her. "Now call your daddy."

She looked at the archaic device with mild distaste. "You think I know his number?"

"Well... yeah." He looked around for back-up. None was forthcoming.

"The only number I know is my own. Why would I need

to remember anyone else's? That's what your contacts are for." She couldn't help her tone. What he was asking was so silly, as if every time she wanted to call someone, she would hand-dial their number like it was the olden days. She knew she shouldn't rile him — she had heard the conversation as she entered the room with Corvo. They were going to kill her. Worse, they were going to give her to that animal in the corner, the one who leered at her through soulless eyes.

Varg.

So that was it, then. Did the fear show on her face? It had to. She had studied the actors on her father's film sets since childhood, fascinated by the way they hid their emotions or emphasized them, the way they conjured tears from nothing. It was a skill she had practiced in front of the mirror many times, and though she had gotten damn good at it, she never had to act under this kind of pressure.

Now, faced with death, she had to project a display of bravado utterly at odds with the churning sensation in the pit of her stomach.

You're doing fine.

"I need my phone," she said.

She watched Baxter's fists clench, saw the subliminal twitch in his eye. "You don't make the orders round here."

She breathed slowly, trying to remain calm. "Then you might as well take me back downstairs, because I don't know the number." She half-smiled. "Unless you want me to guess?"

Stalemate.

Baxter looked her over, drilling his eyes into her. "Where is it?"

"In my schoolbag."

"And where's your schoolbag?"

"Where you left it."

Baxter glanced at Corvo. "Get her bag from the van."

Corvo left the room hurriedly. No one said a word. Baxter locked eyes with Katy, and she stared back, wanting desperately to look anywhere else, but refusing to budge. As a kid, her dad had bought her a dog, a pug she had named Balloon. It was a goofy name, she knew, but he was a goofy dog. Sometimes the pair of them sat on her bed and had staring contests, Balloon's tongue drooping out of the side of his mouth, his enormous eyes never wavering. After a while, she would start to laugh at his funny face, and the pug would emerge victorious.

Balloon the Pug, undefeated staring contest world champion. A king among men.

Now you *must be the pug*, said a voice in her head.

That's the stupidest thing I've ever heard, said another.

Be the pug...

A smile crept onto Katy's face, and she feared she might burst out laughing. Baxter noticed it, his brow furrowing. He looked away in confusion.

With that victory in hand, Katy took the opportunity to look around the room. A reasonably sized kitchen. Baxter sat at a wooden table, scratching between his teeth with a switchblade. Was he trying to intimidate her? No, it was nerves. A bad habit.

He wore a shirt and suit trousers, neatly pressed. A professional, or someone who wants to present themselves to the world as a professional. Someone trying too hard.

Emma leaned against the fridge. With her wig and sunglasses gone, she looked normal. Young, pretty, but over-whelmingly average, the sort of person you'd pass on the street and pay no attention to. It was a better disguise than her ridiculous wig.

Varg got up and moved to the counter, tipping the

contents of a vodka bottle into a metal hip flask, doing it too fast and spilling some. He stole occasional glances at Katy, usually looking at her legs or chest, running his eyes over her. She could smell the alcohol from the other side of the room, and it nauseated her.

The kitchen was sparsely furnished. A table, a couple of chairs with ratty red cushions on them, a two-person sofa, and some white goods; fridge, microwave, cooker. Was any of it useful?

Her eyes settled behind Emma. There, next to an empty bread bin, was the knife rack. There was space for five of the blades, but one was missing. Katy knew where she had last seen it. She tried not to think about it.

Grab one of the knives.

They were too far away.

Be the pug.

The front door closed again, and Corvo came into the room, dumping the blue schoolbag on the table. She reached for it, and Baxter shot out a hand, stopping her.

"Slowly," he said.

She took a long look at him.

Be the pug...

"Why?" she said. "You think I've got a gun?"

Varg laughed, Emma too. Baxter said nothing, but she could hear his teeth grinding over the sound of laughter. He released her wrist, and she unzipped the front pocket of the bag, finding her iPhone 8. She deliberately hadn't upgraded to the latest model, fearing people would think her a show-off. For that reason, she liked to stay several phones behind the trend. According to the lock screen, she had forty-seven unread WhatsApp messages, an unspecified amount of Instagram notifications, and one missed call.

"No fucking around," said Baxter. "Call him."

"What do you want me to say?"

"What do you think? That you're at a goddam sleepover?"

Katy took a deep breath. How far could she push him?

"Okay, I'll just say, *Hi daddy, I've been kidnapped, don't wait up.*"

Corvo chuckled behind her. She could feel his breath on the back of her head.

"She's right," said Emma. "Write it down for her. We want this to be our only contact. Get her to tell him what's happened, then how much we need and where to make the drop-off. Then he never needs to hear your voice."

"That's a good idea," said Varg. He sounded inebriated. "Surprised you didn't think of that, Bax."

"You shut your damn mouth," responded Baxter. "I need paper."

"Try the schoolbag," said Emma.

"Another good idea," muttered Varg.

Baxter shoved his hand into the schoolbag, pulling out a notebook, leafing through it, looking for a blank page. Katy knew the notebook well. Her heart stopped.

Oh god, please don't find it.

Baxter flicked through the pages. It was her math book, the pages filled with equations, sums, graphs and charts, the usual bland school stuff. Except for—

"Wait, what's this?" said Baxter. He looked up from the page, grinning at Katy. "Is this a fucking love letter?"

She didn't answer.

The page was decorated with bubble hearts, one in each corner, carefully shaded. It even smelled of her perfume, which she had sprayed onto the page.

"Read it out," said Varg. He belched. "Maybe it's about me."

"Don't," said Katy, stepping forwards. Corvo put his hands on her shoulders, holding her back.

"*Dearest Jake*," began Baxter, and she wrenched herself free from Corvo's grip and raced towards him, groping wildly for the book.

"Please don't," she said. Baxter shoved her back towards Corvo.

"You've got one fucking job," he spat.

"Sorry," said Corvo, holding onto Katy with a death-grip.

"Now, as I was saying," continued Baxter. "*Dearest Jake.*"

"Stop," said Katy, tears forming. Real ones, this time.

Baxter laughed. So did Varg.

"*I know we have only known each other for a year, but I think I am falling for you. Well ain't that sweet," he said as an aside. "When I'm around you, I can feel my heart beat a little faster.*" He smiled at her. "*You should see a doctor about that.*"

He continued reading. "*Sometimes I lie in bed and I can't sleep, because I'm thinking of you and wondering if you feel the same way too.*"

Shame burned Katy's cheeks.

"That's private," she said.

"Keep reading," said Varg. He had one hand down his bloodstained pants.

"We're wasting time," said Emma.

Corvo said nothing.

"*I know that we're friends, and that makes me so happy. But I'm writing you this letter because I want you to know that I hope, one day, that we can be more than friends.*"

"What is this fucking Romeo and Juliet shit?" laughed Varg. "Just send him a photo of your tits and get it over with."

Baxter looked at Katy, chuckling as tears ran down her crimson cheeks.

"Aw shit, I've embarrassed her." He tore the page from the notebook, crumpled it into a ball, and chucked it in the corner. "Stupid bitch," he muttered, grabbing a pen and getting to work.

"Fuck you," she said.

"Oooooh!" laughed Baxter. "I've really pissed her off." He took her by the chin, raised her head to meet his gaze. "You mad, little girl? Have I upset you? Are you crying?"

She looked past him through blurry eyes, at the knife rack sitting there so invitingly. She could wrestle free, surprise them, grab the knife and bury it in—

No. There were four of them. Even if she stabbed Baxter, the others would get her. She needed to wait. Let them think they had the upper hand, that they had cowed her, beaten her, humiliated her.

Let them believe whatever they want to believe.

She caught Varg's eye. He took a swig from his flask and sneered at her.

Katy curled her own lips into a smile and tipped him a sly wink. Varg squinted at her. He looked confused.

Let them believe whatever they want to believe.

16

———

Katy sat at the table and read over Baxter's scribbled notes. His cursive handwriting was barely legible. As she read, Varg made his way over, taking a seat next to her. She could see Baxter watching him warily.

"Hurry up," said Emma. "It's twenty-five past already."

"Okay," said Baxter. He jabbed the switchblade in Katy's direction. "Call him."

Who was really in charge here, Baxter or Emma? She sensed something between them, and wondered if Varg and Corvo had noticed. Outside, when Katy had head-butted Emma, Baxter had told her she 'still looked good.' There was something about the way he said it that reminded her of when she spoke to Jake, her stomach fluttering with nerves.

Was Baxter in love with Emma?

Well, maybe love was the wrong word, but—

"Call him," snarled Baxter.

She unlocked her phone and opened her contacts, choosing her dad's cell. Now all she had to do was call her father and tell him she had been kidnapped.

Just your typical Saturday.

Varg pulled a pack of cigarettes from his pocket and lit one up, placing the lighter on the table and blowing out a plume of smoke. There was no ashtray, so he tipped the dregs on the floor. The smoke stung Katy's eyes. Under the table, she made sure her leg brushed against Varg's. She felt his gaze fall on her, sensed his bewilderment.

I hope you know what you're doing.

She held the phone to her ear. Her dad was listed in her contacts as Kev, because she knew it wound him up.

She waited.

As she did, her foot found Varg's and lingered there. He flinched, the drooping ash from his cigarette falling to the table. She ran her foot up his leg.

"Hi Dad? It's me. It's Katy."

Baxter nodded, smiled. Varg watched her, the unsmoked cigarette burning to nothing, dangling from his nicotine-stained fingers. He licked his lips.

Katy turned on the tears again.

"Dad... I've been kidnapped."

Everything was proceeding as planned.

Baxter leaned back in his chair, listening to the girl as she spoke to her father. Her *rich* father.

This was it. The way out. A life of petty crime, in and out of jail, and what did he have to show for it? A few scars, some mildly amusing anecdotes, and not a cent to his name.

You have to dream big.

Well, he was living the dream now. Twenty million in cold, hard cash. His life was about to change forever.

"Yes daddy, they want twenty million dollars or... or you'll never see me again."

The girl was crying. Good. As she should be. After all, she was going to die tomorrow. He had made his mind up. She was a liability. She had seen too much.

As Katy rattled off the directions for the drop-off, Baxter couldn't help but grin. Months of planning were finally coming together.

Everything was falling into place.

He looked at the frightened girl, sobbing over the telephone, and wondered why he hadn't done this sooner.

"Please pay them, daddy. I'm so scared. I just want to come home."

She cradled the phone, forcing the last of the tears out.

"I love you," she said. It was the pièce de résistance, the icing on the duplicitous cake.

She put the phone down, sniffed, and turned to Baxter. "He's going to pay."

He shook his head with something approaching awe. "He doesn't even need time. Probably got twenty million in his pocket right now."

"We should've asked for more," said Emma.

Katy could tell Baxter knew she was right. Hell, she knew she was insured for up to *fifty* million in case of kidnapping. These guys were strictly amateurs. They hadn't even listened in on the call.

Thank god. Because if they had, they would have realized she was having a conversation with no one.

Hell, she hadn't even dialed the number.

17

———

Corvo accompanied her back to the cellar.

Things were moving fast. She cursed herself for not buying an extra day to prepare. It would have been easy to do, but she had been thinking on her feet.

When Corvo opened the cellar door, the stench of decay erupted from the sepulchral darkness like an outraged ghost. Katy gagged and took a step back, bumping into Corvo. He, in turn, covered his nose. She looked up at him.

"Please," she said. "Don't make me go down there."

"I have to. There's nowhere else that's safe."

"But..."

"I'm sorry," he said with as much finality as he could muster. "It's just a smell. You'll get used to it."

"That *smell* was my friend," she said angrily. It was not a sentence she ever expected to have to use, and yet there it was, plain as day.

"I know." He spoke quietly, as if ashamed for Varg's actions.

He led her down the stairs. She avoided the third step down, listening as it groaned beneath Corvo's weight.

"Can you at least move her?" she asked.

He sighed like she was being unreasonable. "Fine. I'll put it in the corner."

"*Her.*"

"What?"

"You'll put *her* in the corner. Not *it.*"

He didn't seem to understand the difference. Katy sat on the mattress as he dragged Jill's festering corpse into the shadows.

"That better?"

"I can still smell her," said Katy. "It's getting worse. I saw an air freshener in the bathroom, one of those spray ones. Could you get it for me?"

"I'm sorry," he muttered.

"Please? I think I'll be sick."

"I can't, and that's that. Now lie down."

She lay back as Corvo picked up the rope and wrapped it around her ankles, his tongue poking out the corner of his mouth in concentration. She looked at his t-shirt, at that weird slogan written across his chest.

RESTORE THE SKYWALKER SAGA

"Corvo?" she said.

He grunted in response. "Don't talk to me."

"I just wanna know something," she said.

"I told you to be quiet."

"Just tell me... what's a Skywalker saga?"

The question took him by surprise. He stopped tying her ankles and looked at her. "Don't fool me. You know what that means."

"Is it a band?"

He guffawed, spittle flying from his mouth. "A band? Ha, and people say *I'm* dumb." He sat heavily on the mattress, making himself comfortable. "You've seen *Star Wars,* right?"

She hadn't, but nodded anyway.

"Best series ever," said Corvo. "Am I right?"

"The best," she smiled.

"And what about *The Last Jedi?*"

Katy sensed there was a definite right and wrong answer to the question, but she didn't know which Corvo wanted to hear. She tried to think. All she knew about *Star Wars* was that she had met Adam Driver at one of her dad's parties. He was very nice, and very tall.

She shrugged, and said, "Are you kidding me? *The Last Jedi?*"

Corvo laughed. "Exactly," he said, not letting her finish. "A total betrayal."

"A betrayal," repeated Katy, nodding sagely. "Boy, it sure was."

"Exactly!"

Katy had never seen him so animated. He sounded like an excitable child.

"I mean, *The Force Awakens* was the best film ever made, right?"

She nodded again. "Definitely."

He smirked. "Wrong," he said, wagging a finger. "Actually, *The Last Jedi* would have been the best film ever made, if someone else had made it. You see—"

What the fuck is he talking about?

Katy smiled and nodded in all the right places, though it was hard to keep up. Often he would ask a rhetorical question, and when she agreed, he would correct her.

"Well, actually..."

"Actually..."

"You'd think! But actually..."

It was impossible to listen to.

"So my friend Chad started this online petition," he

continued, pointing to his shirt. She sensed the story was coming to an end. God, it had to be! "We've got almost 2,000 signatures so far. If they can re-do *Justice League,* then Disney can damn well show *Star Wars* the respect it deserves."

Katy realized it was her turn to speak. He was saying something about a petition? "Yeah," she said, playing it safe.

Corvo smiled. "It's nice to talk to someone about this. None of the guys upstairs know what I'm talking about."

"Yeah," she smiled. "I love those Marvel films."

Corvo froze. His voice dropped to a hushed, outraged whisper.

"You... *what?*"

Shit shit shit shit shit

She'd said the wrong thing. She had no idea what the right thing was, but it was definitely *not* that. Wasn't that what they were talking about? Disney movies?

She smiled coyly and playfully tapped him on the arm. "I'm joking, silly."

Corvo's grim features loosened. "Oh man, you got me there. Thought I was gonna have to kill you!"

She laughed with him, not knowing if he meant it.

"Can't you leave my feet untied? I get so sore lying here."

He seemed to consider it. "I can't. I'm sorry. You're a nice girl, but I can't. Bax wouldn't let me."

"And you do what he says, right?"

"Yeah. He's the boss. Smartest guy I ever met."

"But do you trust him?"

Indecision flickered across Corvo's face. "Yeah. I mean, why wouldn't I?"

"No reason. It's just... I heard him say something behind your back."

"Bullshit."

Katy shrugged. "You're probably right."

Corvo looked at her uncertainly. He finished the knot and waited. He was thinking. "What did he say?" he asked.

"I don't know, I didn't hear." She waited a moment. "Something about how twenty million divides by three."

"But there are four of us."

"That's what I thought." She held her wrists out in front of her and, without thinking, Corvo started to tie them. "He was saying it to the woman. I thought it was weird."

"It *is* weird."

"How long have you known each other?"

"Not long. Only met Bax a few months ago."

It's working. He's buying it.

He looked at her intently.

"You think he's gonna kill Varg?"

Jesus H Christ.

"Varg was in the room," she said. "All three of them were. It was when you went to get my bag."

"You gotta be wrong," he said. "Must've been talking about something else."

"Maybe you're right."

He finished tying the knot, barely registering what he was doing.

"He really said that?"

Katy nodded. Corvo's face fell dark.

"It smells so bad," she said. "Bring me the air freshener from the bathroom... please?"

"Sure," he said, only half-listening.

"It'll be fine," said Katy. "I'm sure he didn't mean anything by it."

"Yeah." He turned to leave.

"Corvo?"

"What?"

She batted her eyelids. "The air-freshener. Please bring it."

"I will."

Then he climbed the stairs and left.

He returned shortly, the spray can clutched in his oversized paw. It did little to mask the stench, the pinewood scent mingling with the rotten odor, creating a new, somehow *more* foul smell. Corvo didn't say a word. As he headed for the stairs, she called out to him.

"Can you just leave it here?"

He looked at the can, unsure.

"Come on," she said, "there's not much I can do with *that*."

"Guess so," he mumbled, and handed it to her. At the foot of the stairs, he paused, his back to her. "Me and Bax are going to get the money tomorrow. If it's all there, you can go free. I promise."

"Thank you," she said softly. She believed he meant it, though she knew it wasn't up to him.

"When we're gone... watch out for Varg."

"What do you mean?"

"It's just... me and Bax, we keep him in line. Tomorrow, there'll be just him and Emma." He paused. "She can't watch him all the time."

With that, he strode up the stairs, the door closing behind him. She heard the key in the lock, and then all was quiet. She thought about what Corvo had said.

Watch out for Varg.

He would be down here at the first opportunity. As soon as Emma's back was turned, he would be here, watching her, touching her...

Good.

That was what she wanted.

Everything was proceeding according to plan.

18

<hr>

With her hands in front of her, untying the ropes around her ankles was easy. Corvo's knots were like shoelaces, coming apart with one simple tug. She got up, wandering across the room, keeping her legs moving. They hurt from her midnight dash the night before, but she couldn't let them freeze up on her. She tried the panels across the window, but the new wood was dry and immovable.

A bundle of fishing rods remained in the corner, but she was unlikely to defend herself with a long, bendy stick. She checked the stairs, testing the wood on the third step down. She could detect a hairline crack in the center, but there was no way to tell when it would eventually break. It could last for months, and she had less than twenty four hours. They were due to make the pick-up at twelve noon the next day — Sunday, she reminded herself — at a rural gas station. She had no idea where it was in relation to the building she was currently in, but figured it would have to be far away, at least an hour's drive. When they discovered the money wasn't coming, the shit would hit the fan. She had until that precise moment. But how would she know the time? With no light visible through the windows, it could be morning, afternoon, or evening. She would have to listen for them going to bed, then hopefully wake in time to hear them leaving in the morning.

There were too many ifs, too many buts.

She went back to the mattress and tried to rest, but sleep was not forthcoming.

In a matter of hours, either she would be dead... or they would be.

19

———

"WHERE'S CORVO?" ASKED BAXTER.

Emma glanced up from her paperback. "Gone to bed."

Baxter nodded. The two of them were alone in the kitchen. The pistol lay next to Emma on the armrest of the sofa.

"What about Varg?"

This time Emma didn't even look up. "In his room. I heard him jerking off."

"Jesus."

"He definitely wasn't jerking off Jesus."

Baxter sighed. The longest two days of his life were almost over. "Watch him closely tomorrow. I don't want him going near the Ketcher girl until we get the money."

"I can handle it," she said icily. "Varg's afraid of women he can't fuck."

Footsteps shuffled along the hall. Baxter knew who it was before the door opened. Corvo lumbered with the subtlety of a rhino, but Varg... Varg *crept*.

The door groaned open and the thin man entered.

"Oh for fuck's sake," said Baxter. Varg wore nothing but

filthy white underpants, his scrawny frame surprisingly taut with muscle. He paid them no attention, going straight to the gas oven, the scent of stale sex wafting through the air. He pulled a cigarette from the waistband of his briefs.

"Oh, you are *not* gonna smoke that," said Baxter.

"Want one?" grinned Varg. He twisted the dial on the cooker, a thin blue flame appearing on the hob. He leaned over and lit his cigarette with it, then turned to Baxter. "I got plenty more where this came from. Just can't find my lighter."

"We've not seen it," said Emma.

"Well," he drawled, "If you do, you know where to find me." He walked past them again, and Baxter held his breath. Varg flashed them his red teeth. "You might wanna knock, though. Can't stop thinking 'bout the girly downstairs."

"She's *sixteen*," said Baxter.

"She's legal in some states," said Varg. "But don't worry, I won't let that spoil my fun."

"Stay the fuck away from her," said Emma. "Once we've got the money, she's all yours. But until then, keep your paws off."

Varg looked at her for a long time. "Whatever happens... happens," he said. He took a draw on his cigarette and left the room, the smoke lingering.

Baxter waved it away. He felt a migraine coming on. Though he no longer cared what Varg did to the girl, he would still rather not know the details. Ignorance is bliss, after all.

He glanced at Emma, trying to play it cool. "Why is he even here?"

"Corvo said he'd be useful."

"And when will that begin?"

She laughed. Emma didn't laugh often, and when she

did, it was usually at his expense, but now she was laughing *with* him. His heart beat a little faster.

"Want a drink?" he said.

Emma folded the page of her paperback and closed it. "Fine."

Baxter leaped to his feet.

Slow down. You look too keen.

He stalked towards the kitchen counter. Never before had he been so acutely aware of his gait.

"What the hell are you doing?" asked Emma as he kneeled on the counter and groped around above the hanging cupboards.

"I hid something here," he said. "Was gonna save it for tomorrow, but I... ah! Found it." He lifted a bottle of champagne down, then collected two cracked pint glasses from the cupboard, arranging them on the counter. "Champagne, madam?" he said in a feeble French accent.

"You trying to get me drunk?"

He was.

"Not at all," he said, emptying the bottle into the glasses, the bubbles spilling over the rims. "But I don't think we'll have much time to celebrate tomorrow. Once Ketcher pays, I wanna split."

Emma pushed herself up from the sofa. She crossed the kitchen and accepted the glass from Baxter.

"Oh shit," he said, grimacing.

"What?"

He pointed at the sofa. "I think you sat in Corvo's sandwich."

She followed his gaze to the patch of smeared mayonnaise on the cushion where moments before she had been lounging.

"Goddam," she said, patting her ass, her hands coming

away sticky. "That fucking slob." She started to unbuckle her belt.

"What are you doing?" asked Baxter.

She glared at him. "I'm gonna wash my jeans in the basin. You got a problem with that?"

"No problem," he smiled, watching as she kicked off her sneakers and slid her jeans over her hips.

God bless you, Corvo, and your disgusting eating habits!

Emma scowled at him. "You're pathetic, you know that? You're like a teenager getting his first sniff of pussy." She stumbled slightly, grabbing Baxter's arm to maintain her balance. They locked eyes. "Don't get excited," she said, shaking her head.

"What you guys doing?"

Baxter turned to the door. He hadn't heard it open.

It was Corvo.

"Don't you know how to fucking *knock?*" snarled Emma, her jeans around her ankles.

Corvo's eyes darted from Emma's flushed face to Baxter and back again.

"Sorry," he said quietly. "I just came to get a drink." He glanced down at Emma's underwear and took a step back. "Guess I'll leave you to it."

"Yeah, I guess you should," said Emma.

Corvo waited. He started to say something, then seemed to change his mind.

"What are you waiting for?" said Baxter. "Get the fuck outta here!"

"Yeah, okay," mumbled Corvo. "Sorry."

He hesitated another moment, then walked slowly away, leaving the door wide open. Baxter listened to his lumbering steps receding down the hallway.

"Did you see the way he looked at us?" said Emma.

"You're not wearing pants," said Baxter. "Can you blame him?"

Emma stared at the door like she expected him to reappear. "It was more than that," she said. "He looked... suspicious. I didn't like it."

"You think he's up to something?"

She didn't answer.

Instead, she stepped fully out of her jeans and crossed to the basin. She turned on the faucet and dumped her jeans in.

"I didn't like the way he looked at us," she said. "I didn't like it at all."

20

———

Be the pug.

Katy couldn't get those words out of her head. What was that thing her father did, that phrase he repeated whenever he was stressed?

A mantra.

That was it, a mantra. She supposed *be the pug* was her own personal mantra, and despite the stupidity of it, the sentiment rang true. And hey, it actually worked.

It calmed her.

She lay on the mattress, listening to the sounds of the lodge. The groan of water surging through rusted pipes, the faint sound of the wood settling. There were occasional footsteps leading to the bathroom, and sometimes it would even flush. But not always.

When the gulls started to squawk outside, she figured it must be morning. On cue, the building came alive. Music played from a radio. People talked, Corvo's voice booming throughout the hallway. He appeared a little while later and helped her to the bathroom without a word. When they returned, he retied her bonds in silence.

"You okay?" she asked softly.

"Yeah."

"You don't sound it."

Taking a chance, she put her hand on his arm. He didn't seem to notice.

"It's just," he said, "I've been thinking, you know?"

She nodded sympathetically. She had been doing a lot of thinking herself.

"What about?"

"About what you said. About the money."

Good. That's what I wanted you to think about.

He cleared his throat. "I, uh, walked in on Bax and Emma last night. They were..." His cheeks turned crimson.

"I knew it," said Katy.

"You did?" He looked genuinely shocked.

"Have you ever been in love, Corvo?" she asked.

He shook his head sadly. "No. Ain't nobody could love a guy like me. Why?"

"It's the way Baxter and Emma look at each other." Her voice dropped to a conspiratorial whisper. *"They're in love."*

She was bullshitting him. She had no idea if that's how they behaved, but she definitely had an inkling that Baxter harbored a crush on Emma. If what Corvo had said was true — and why wouldn't it be? — then things were working out better than she had hoped. She had wanted to plant a seed of doubt in Corvo's mind, and already the seed was sprouting.

She offered a wry smile. "God, it all makes sense now."

"What does?" He stopped tying her wrists, the ropes falling forgotten to the floor.

She laughed softly. "It's probably nothing."

"No, what? Tell me."

She hesitated, playing it up. Manipulating Corvo was almost too easy.

"It's just... I heard them last night. In the hall."

He leaned in close. "What did they say?"

"I couldn't make out everything." The lie she had been rehearsing all night tumbled easily out. "But Baxter said something about him and Emma moving to Barbados."

"Barbados? Why would they go to Italy?"

"Umm, yeah, that's what I thought," said Katy. She had prepared herself for every direction the conversation could take, but hadn't counted on Corvo's ignorance of geography. "Anyway, Emma said that with fifteen million, they could buy their own island."

Corvo smiled at the thought. "That's not a bad idea. Maybe I'll do that."

"Don't you see, though? Fifteen million... between the two of them..." She waited for him to join the dots. It wasn't enough. Trying not to reveal her frustration, she added, "And then Baxter said he wondered what Varg would do with his *five* million."

"Ha, Varg'll spend it on hookers and blow," said Corvo.

For god's sake, listen to me!

"But Corvo... don't you understand? Fifteen million, plus five million, is *twenty million*. What does that leave you?"

He fell silent. "Wait a minute..."

Katy smiled sweetly. "I'm sure it was a mistake."

"Hey Corvo, you ready to go?"

Baxter's voice, calling from the kitchen. Corvo looked at Katy, his face a mask of fury, and also, she thought, hurt.

"But Emma's my friend," he said. "She wouldn't do that to me."

"People do crazy things when they're in love," she said.

"Corvo! Hurry the fuck up!"

"I better go," he said, reaching for the rope, quickly tying it in his usual basic knot, once over her ankles, once over her wrists. "I'm coming," he shouted up the stairs. Then he stood, nibbling on a fingernail and gazing at Katy. "Thank you," he said.

She nodded. "Be careful, Corvo."

You bastard.

The door slammed, and she listened as they went about their business. Outside, an engine sputtered into life, and then the van was off, the sound fading into the velvet crash of the waves.

Baxter and Corvo were gone. For how long? She was planning on asking Corvo, but it had taken him an eternity to get his head around what she was saying...

Suddenly the reality of the situation crashed down around her. She had sent them off on a wild goose chase. There was no money... no one knew she was kidnapped. What would they do when they returned empty handed? Torture her? Kill her? What was she playing at? She was almost out of time. Why, oh *why* hadn't she bought herself another day and told them that the pick-up couldn't be until Monday? Or even just called her dad, like she could so easily have done? He would have paid, and the insurance would have covered it.

Because of Jill. Because of what they did to her... and what they'll do to you.

Yes. That was why. This was no longer about the easy way out, or doing the sensible thing. There was one word on Katy Ketcher's mind, and one word alone...

Revenge.

Be the pug.

She reached down to her ankles, finding the knot. As expected, it came away easily. She remembered the time she had crawled up behind Jill in school and tied her shoelaces together while she spoke with some boy. It had been so simple, and when Jill casually walked away, she had fallen straight into him, head-butting his chest and landing on her knees. Jill had been so mad that day... and then, later on, they had gone for ice-cream together and laughed about it, everything forgiven, all anger and resentment forgotten.

Katy looked at Jill's body rotting in the corner. She was beginning to get used to the smell now, and she found the very notion horrific.

"This is for you, Jill," she said to her friend. "I'm sorry for all the times I was mean to you."

Memories flooded her brain, but she pushed them away and got to her feet, stepping gently from side to side to get her blood flowing. Using her teeth, she undid the rope around her wrists and walked clumsily towards the wooden stairs on throbbing legs. The first thing she did was check the third step from the top. She had investigated it before, but now she had something different in mind. Could she prise it up? If the wood was as rotten as the planks that had covered the windows, then maybe...

She planted her feet on either side of the step and gripped it in her small fingers, pulling on it. Despite her awkward pose, it seemed to be working. One side raised, the long nails slipping free of the damp wood. She adjusted her position, trying the other side. It came free with a minimum of effort. The plank was heavy, the nails protruding from both ends. What could she do with it, though?

Katy's heart stopped.

She heard movement.

Someone was there. Too late, she saw the shadow of their feet in the gap beneath the door, and then the key was in the lock.

Standing motionless at the top of the stairs, she had nowhere to hide.

21

THE LOCK TURNED SLOWLY, TENTATIVELY, AS IF WHOEVER WAS behind the door didn't want anyone else to know. Katy dropped the wood back into place and scurried down the steps, taking two at a time, jumping the last three and landing heavily. She threw herself onto the mattress, almost bouncing off it, scrabbling for the rope, wrapping it round her ankles, once, twice, then tying it.

The handle rattled, the door inching open, yellow light invading the room like the rising sun.

She finished the knot. It was shoddy, but did it look like Corvo's handiwork? Katy thought it did. There was no time for her wrists.

"Hey, girly."

She looked up at Varg as he stepped inside, carefully shutting the door so as not to alert Emma. He started down the stairs. For a moment his foot hovered above the third step. He switched, avoiding it. "Gotta watch that one," he said. "Gonna break one of these days."

He made his way down unhurriedly.

"You don't look so good," he said, the noxious alcohol fumes from his breath reaching her long before he did.

"I don't feel well."

He took a seat on the mattress. "Didn't come here to listen to you complain."

"Why did you, then?"

He ignored the question, taking the hip-flask from his pocket, unscrewing the cap. "Want some?"

She shook her head. "No, sir."

"Sir?" Varg grinned and slugged down some of the alcohol. "I like that. I could get used to that." He patted her knee, his eyes traveling up her body. "You got your hands free?"

She nodded. "The ropes hurt."

"They're meant to. Life hurts. You understand?"

"No, sir."

His lizard tongue darted out across his lips. "Didn't think so. You're too young, too stupid." He took another drink. "How old are you, girly?"

"Sixteen."

"Yeah, that sounds right. You're a little bitch." He moved closer, sniffed the air. "Smell like one too."

He repulsed her, but she did everything in her power not to show it.

"I don't want to die, Varg," she said. "That *is* your name, isn't it?"

"That's my name, don't wear it out," he snickered.

She pretended to smile at that. "Can I call you Varg?"

"I preferred it when you called me sir."

"Okay." She took a deep breath. "I don't want to die... sir."

"That's better." He patted her thigh, his hand lingering too long before he placed it back in his lap. "Everyone dies, you know."

"I know. My mom died when I was little."

Varg snorted. "I hardly knew my mom. Ran off when I was a kid, left me with that bastard." He took out his cigarettes and shoved one in his mouth, then searched his pockets. "Damn lighter," he muttered.

"Did you not like your dad?"

"Like him? I killed him."

Katy gasped.

Varg shook his head. "Don't give me that. He tried to kill me first. Came at me with a fucking ashtray. He was old, and I was young. Never underestimate kids, y'know? Boys, anyway. They ain't *that* stupid. They know how to fight, they know how to kill. And yeah, sure, maybe I wasn't the smartest kid, but I was a quick learner. Someone comes at you with a weapon, you find a bigger one. I can still remember the noise his skull made when I hit him with the chair leg. *Pop!* And his face... you shoulda seen his face. You wanna know the best part? He actually started *crying*. Oh, he never cried when he beat my mom so bad she went to hospital, or when he broke my leg, or my arm, or my shoulder. But when his own time was up, he cried like a little baby. It was pathetic. You know what I did to him as he lay there?"

Katy shook her head.

"I pulled his pants down. That might sound weird, but that's what I did. I pulled his pants down, and I got the chair leg, and I—"

"Stop," said Katy. "Please."

He looked at her and chuckled.

"I know what you're thinking. You're thinking I'm gonna do that to you, right?"

What response was he looking for? What would be the

best thing to say in this situation? Katy's kidnapping training hadn't prepared her for *this*.

"No," she whispered.

Varg's jaw clenched. "Yes, you are. Don't *lie* to me. All my life, people have lied to me. Why don't you just tell me the truth, goddammit? Now tell me, is that what you were thinking?"

Her heart jackhammered. She couldn't think straight. He slapped her across the face. "Answer me!"

"Yes! Yes, that's what I was thinking!" she cried. It hadn't been, but it sure as hell was now.

Varg cracked his knuckles. "Yes, what?"

"Yes, sir."

He laughed at that, long and hard.

"You scared, girly?"

"Yes. Yes, sir."

"You should be. You're going to die."

"I know," she said quietly. "I don't want to, but I know I am."

"I'm gonna be the one to do it. Did you know *that*?"

"I suspected."

"*I suspected*. Christ, you rich cunts are all the same. *I suspected*. Fuck, I need a smoke." He sipped from the flask, then pressed it towards her. "Drink," he commanded.

She took the flask and drank, the liquid burning the walls of her throat. It was her first taste of alcohol, and she didn't like it.

"Good, huh?" he said.

"No."

He laughed again, his eyes returning to her legs. Her heart wouldn't slow down. She had to take back the power, or are least some of it. If not, he was going to do something. She could feel it.

"If you're going to kill me," she began, "there's something I want you to know. Something I've never told anyone."

He looked at her, intrigued. "What?"

"Wait a second," she said. She reached behind the mattress and found the can of air freshener. Varg visibly tensed. She aimed it towards the corner, towards Jill, and fired off a burst of forest pine. "It smells so bad," she said, placing the canister next to her on the mattress.

"Where'd you get that?" he asked.

"Corvo brought it for me."

He watched her for a long time, unmoving. "You fuck Corvo?"

"No," she said, looking him in the eyes. They were blue, the most intense eyes she'd ever seen. And cold, so very cold, like two icy pools.

"You'd better not have fucked him."

"That's what I'm trying to tell you," she said.

"What?" He trailed a finger up her calf. "Come on, then. Lemme hear your last words."

She watched his hand inch its way up her leg. His touch made her want to vomit.

"I'm a virgin," she said.

"So what?" said Varg, trying to act aloof, but giving the game away by licking his lips again with his horrifically restless tongue.

"I don't want to die a virgin."

Varg nodded in slow motion. When he opened his mouth, his lips smacked together. He scratched at his neck.

"What... why are you, uh, telling me this?"

Katy saw the change in his behavior, watched him squirm. It emboldened her.

"I'm just saying... I don't want to die a virgin... *sir.*"

"In the kitchen," he said, "you knew what you were

doing, right? With your foot? You kept touching me. Trying to turn me on."

"That's right."

"What about when you winked at me?"

Jesus, Varg, keep up.

"That was for you. I couldn't say anything in front of the others, but..."

He swallowed, his hands closing over her calf. "You know, I jerked off to you all night."

Oh god.

"Really?" she said, like that was the ultimate compliment every girl wanted to hear.

"Yeah. It was good. *Real* good." He smiled at her. "I'm red raw down there."

It was the most revolting sentence Katy had ever heard, but she couldn't stop now. She had him, a worm squirming on a hook. Her body trembled with nerves. She tried not to show it.

"Please, sir," she said, opening her eyes as wide as they would go. "Will you be my first?"

His leering grin broadened. "Girly, I'll be your first *and* your last."

He moved forwards, his hand sliding further up her leg, past her knee and towards the hem of her skirt. She recoiled, pulling her leg away.

"Wait," she said, trying to smile. "What's the rush? I want to show you something first."

He panted at her like a dog in heat. She wanted to cry. He was a monster, and here she was trying to *seduce* him. She had read about situations like this online, about the way women react to frightening men with politeness and submission. She hadn't really understood it at the time.

If someone touched me, I'd just punch them, she remembered telling Jill.

… Jill…

But now she realized she couldn't. He was so much stronger than her. Could he tell she was scared? Probably. She imagined he got off on it. It was a power trip.

"So?" said Varg. He rubbed at his crotch, apparently unaware he was doing so. "What you wanna show me?"

She stretched forwards, untying her ankles. He didn't stop her.

This had better work.

"What are you doing?" he rasped, his authority dwindling.

"I want you to sit back and enjoy the show."

Was that sexy? Or cheesy? She didn't know. This was unfamiliar territory. It was true, she *was* a virgin. Not only that, but she had only kissed one boy before, Charles O'Connor, and that hardly counted. He had tried to slip her the tongue at a party, and she had gagged, then laughed, then run away. It wasn't that she didn't think about boys. She did, sometimes. But usually she would rather spend time with Jill, or by herself.

She started to unbutton her blouse.

"You like this?" she breathed.

"Yes."

"Call me ma'am."

"Yes, ma'am," said Varg.

She rested her head back and bit her bottom lip theatrically as the first button came free. Varg reached out, and she shook her head.

"No. Your turn soon. For now, just watch."

"Yes, ma'am." He put one hand down his jeans and rummaged around. God, she *hated* him.

"I like when you touch yourself," she lied. "Do you want to see me touch myself?"

"Yeah," he managed, his breath coming in wheezing gasps. "Yes, ma'am. Girly, I want to see your pussy."

"Soon," she said.

She unfastened the next button on her blouse, and then the next, until she was able to slide one hand in and cup her breast. She ran her other hand through her hair.

Jesus, I need a shampoo, she thought.

"Mmmmm," she groaned, as she slipped her hand into her bra, never feeling more gross than she did at that moment.

Varg was masturbating. Horrified, Katy looked away from him.

"Yeah, you bitch, you little horny bitch, you turn me on," he said, fumbling in his pocket for a smoke with his free hand, placing it between his chapped lips. She needed him to look away, just for a moment, but his eyes were glued to her chest.

Varg patted his pockets. "Where's my fucking lighter?" he mumbled, his face scrunched up like it had been left in the sun too long.

Katy's heartbeat was wildly out-of-control.

She spread her legs slightly. Varg's gaze dropped to her waist.

Now!

Her right hand glided from her hair to the air freshener as her left hand pulled something from her bra.

Varg briefly glanced at the gold, metallic object she was holding.

"Hey, that's my lighter," he said, as Katy flipped the cap and ignited it, swinging the air-freshener in an arc, stopping right in front of the lighter. She saw Varg's eyes widen as he realized what was happening.

"Go to hell," she spat, and squeezed the nozzle of the canister.

22

THE VAPOUR TOUCHED THE FLAME, IGNITING ON CONTACT.

A ball of blue fire erupted in Varg's face. He threw himself backwards, screaming wretchedly. Katy followed, the makeshift flamethrower held out in front of her. Varg raised his hands to protect his face, his skin sizzling and blackening before Katy's eyes. He scrambled back, kicking out wildly, his foot connecting with her calf. Katy fell hard, winding herself and losing her grip on the air freshener. It rattled across the floor, out of reach.

"Fucking bitch," shouted Varg. His voice was a gargled mess, his face a foul kaleidoscope of oozing colors. Patches of dark, melted skin flapped from his chin and cheeks, exposing the red muscle beneath. He looked like a monster, inhuman, staggering towards her. A terrible thought hit Katy.

She would have to finish him off.

Turning from him, she scurried away on hands and knees, searching for the canister. It was close. She stretched a hand out, her fingers grazing the metal, and then he was on her, grunting and spitting. She spun beneath him, looking up into what was left of his face. The skin bubbled, and his right eye was gone, yellow mucus oozing down his cheek.

"I'll kill you," he said through crispy lips that reminded Katy of overdone strips of bacon.

He closed his hands around her throat, tightening them, crushing her windpipe. She battered her fists against them, digging her nails into his fingers, trying to prise them up. No use. He was too strong. Varg's grip tightened. It was a pain unlike anything Katy had ever experienced.

Was this how Jill felt when Varg was stabbing her, slicing her up, gutting her? Katy's vision blurred, her life ebbing away to nothing but a memory in the grieving brain of her father.

Be the pug.

She couldn't. He was so big. She couldn't...

Be.

The.

Pug.

She thought of her father trying to clean Balloon the Pug's ears, and the way the small dog had fought back, scratching his little paws at her dad's face and howling.

Try it.

Why not? She had nothing left to lose.

Varg's wretched features were contorted into a savage grin, and Katy raised a shaking hand to his face and dug her nails in. His skin sizzled like a s'more, burning her fingers. But the pain was fleeting. She jammed the fingers of her other hand deep into his flesh. Varg's toasted lips drew back in sneering pain.

Then Katy yanked her hands away and the blackened skin tore free.

Varg roared in agony. It was like a chemical peel, but

stripping the skin down to pink muscle and gleaming white bone. He toppled backwards, releasing her, and Katy shuffled away, choking. She could hardly breathe, tears streaming down her cheeks. Varg sat up, clutching his horrific face, gasping raggedly. Blood gushed from between his fingers, running in thick rivers down his arms. He forced himself to his feet.

"Why won't you die?" she whispered, rubbing at the contusions on her neck. Still he came for her, his face a ruin, his eyes two craters set into a scalding, desolate moon.

"I'ma... kill... you..." he slurred, lunging forwards.

Easily side-stepping his clumsy movements, Katy ran for the stairs. With an aching weariness, Varg followed her. Katy moved on autopilot. She climbed the stairs, pausing near the top to lift the loose plank. Varg's blood-soaked hand found the rail, and he started after her.

Katy raised the plank. Two long, rusted nails jutted out from the underside.

"You killed Jill," she snarled, and brought the wooden step down across Varg's head.

The plank smacked hard against him. His body jerked stiffly, his throat emitting a nightmarish rattle.

"Girly," he sighed, and then he fell backwards, taking the plank with him, his head slapping against the floor like a saturated sponge, spraying blood in a three-foot radius.

Katy watched as his leg spasmed. Smoke rose from his skull, the smell of burning meat filling the air.

"Was that good for you?" she said, and cracked a deranged half-smile.

23

Emma stepped out of the shower, wrapping a towel around her waist.

Damn those men. Months of preparation, of going over plans, of thinking everything through to the smallest detail... and they had forgotten to bring towels. There was beer all right, a fridge full of the stuff, but no fucking fresh *towels*. The one she was using had been here when they arrived, rigid and crusted, and no amount of soaking in water seemed to soften it. She dried herself as best she could — it was like rubbing her skin with sandpaper — and dressed in her jeans and vest. She hadn't brought any other clothes. It was all evidence, and she thought it best to leave nothing behind when they moved on. Once the reward money came through, she could buy all the expensive designer shit she wanted.

Water dripped from her hair, and she glanced at her watch. Quarter-past-nine. They had been gone less than twenty minutes, and already she was getting antsy. The thought of all that money, that glorious, wonderful money... and all that stood between her and five million dollars were a few hours with Varg. She could deal with that. Varg was a sleazy piece of shit, but so was she, in the right frame of mind.

She tucked the gun into her jeans and left the downstairs bathroom, her wet feet padding across the wooden floor. Halfway along the hallway, she froze.

"Shit."

The cellar door was wide open.

Varg was at it again. She supposed it didn't matter. They would have the money soon, and the girl was going to die anyway, but still, he could have at least *waited*.

It was just good manners.

She made her way towards the door, a strange feeling of trepidation settling over her. Footprints led away from the cellar, small and red. They sure as hell didn't belong to Varg.

"You dumb bastard," she said, heading into the cellar and hurrying down the stairs. She caught herself at the last second, her foot hovering over the missing third step.

"Oh, you think you're so clever," she smiled, stepping over the gap.

The girl had escaped once, and they had found her. It would be just as easy second time around.

Except it wouldn't.

Because this time Baxter and Corvo had the van, and wouldn't be back for hours. She and Varg would have to give chase on foot. It was fine, she told herself. They would catch her. She couldn't have gone far. She was—

That was when Emma saw him.

Varg, lying unmoving on his back, a plank of wood jutting out from the top of his head. She took a few steps closer and saw the ghoulish skeletal face framed by charred skin. He was dead. The girl had killed him.

Varg, butchered by a schoolgirl.

Emma smiled. She was impressed. The little girl was surprisingly resourceful. It would make killing her that much sweeter.

But first, she had to *find* her.

Emma raced back up the stairs, gazing down at the bloody footprints that led through the hallway. She shook her head. The foolish bitch wasn't as clever as she'd thought after all. She had left a perfect trail to follow. Oddly, the prints didn't go to towards the front door, instead heading towards the stairs that led to the second floor. It made sense. The front door was locked, always was, and the girl must have known that.

Emma followed the trail, the prints growing fainter until they reached the stairs. The girl's only chance would be to escape out one of the upstairs windows. Had she been upstairs before? Emma wondered if Corvo — that soft-headed clown — had taken her to the bathroom up there. She cautiously climbed the stairs.

Emma was not a nervous woman. The day of the kidnapping had felt like any other day. It was just a job, another nine-to-five at the office, and yet now an unfamiliar feeling of anxiety swam through her head.

She reached the top of the stairs. The hallway forked, two rooms to the left, three to the right. Emma smiled. There, on the wall, was a bloodstain. A couple of finger-prints. The girl was clever, sure... but not *that* clever. Leaving a mark like that was a rookie mistake. Emma hastened down the hall. There was another stain further down.

"Might as well have drawn me a fucking map," she said.

The bathroom door was ajar, one last tell-tale mark near the handle. Emma threw the door open and stepped into the room. The shower curtain was drawn, and she pulled the gun from her jeans, thumbing the safety, pointing it towards the curtain. Heart thumping, she grabbed the curtain, pulling it so hard it ripped from the rail, falling into the rancid brown bathwater.

There was no one behind it.

Adrenaline coursed through her veins.

"Get a hold of yourself," she said, her eyes darting to the open window. It was small, but the girl could fit through. Sunlight streamed in through the gap, and Emma poked her head out, scanning the landscape. She would be easy to spot amongst the sand and dry, grassy dunes.

"I'm coming to get you, bitch!" she shouted, too preoccupied to notice the movement behind her, the revolting bathwater shifting, bubbling, a skull-shaped dome breaking the surface.

Emma, guided by rage, held the gun out the window, squeezing off a shot that echoed for miles.

Behind her, two black, dripping hands emerged from the water, gripping the handles of the tub.

Emma took a step backwards. A reflection in the window caught her eye, a dark, inhuman shape. It opened its eyes and met her gaze, and then it was moving. Emma whirled, but she was too slow. The creature stepped onto the edge of the bath and leaped towards her. She tried to raise the gun but the shapeless figure slammed into her. She fell backwards, her spine crunching against the ceramic cistern lid, the jolt sending the gun clattering to the linoleum. Black goop slid oil-like from the face of the creature, revealing pale, human flesh beneath.

The girl.

She stank, an acrid odor of sewer-filth, the foul gunk in the bath having festered there for Christ-knows how long. A stringy glob landed on Emma's face as the girl raised her fist, bringing it down hard. The blow struck true, right where the girl had headbutted her the day before, but Emma was no stranger to pain.

The girl clambered on top of her, reaching for the gun, the dark liquid dripping from her arm like a melting popsicle.

Emma shoved her backwards, the girl's head hitting the floor with a vicious *thud*. She grabbed the gun, but the girl was already up, lunging at her, trying to wrestle the gun free. Emma squeezed the trigger, the shot deafening as the bullet whistled past the girl's face, slamming into the wood and leaving a smoldering, circular hole. The girl grabbed her by the throat and pushed away from the wall, the two of them tumbling towards the bath. Emma braced herself for the impact as her shoulder jarred against the lip of the tub. She held the gun as the pair grappled for control, struggling to aim at the girl, who sneered at her through the sludge with a crazed, maniacal look on her young face, her teeth bared, eyes wide.

"Let go," screamed Emma. It was unlike her to lose her cool, but this girl was dangerous. She had already killed Varg. The girl pounded her face with one fist, Emma weathering each blow, focusing on the deadly weapon in her hand. She twisted her wrist, angled it towards the girl, and fired again. The bullet grazed the girl's shoulder. She barely reacted.

"What the fuck is wrong with you?" said Emma as the girl doubled her efforts. She stopped hitting Emma, instead stabbing her nails into her wrists. She raked them down Emma's arm, peeling up deep troughs of skin, hot blood bubbling quickly to the surface and spraying the yellowing wall.

The bitch wasn't about to give up, but neither was

Emma. She flicked her wrist and threw the gun into the bathwater.

If she couldn't use it, no one would.

Not that it mattered. She would kill the girl with her bare hands. She would rip her fucking eyeballs out of her skull and shit in the sockets. The girl, either out of instinct or ignorance, plunged her hands into the muck, searching for a weapon that almost certainly wouldn't fire, and Emma took her opportunity. She put her hand on the back of the girl's head and slammed her face-first against the tub. The girl yelped, and for a moment, Emma remembered she was dealing with a little girl.

A child.

Emma's mothering instinct, however, had long since withered and died. Killing a child was easier than killing an adult. She had done it before, and she would do it again, if this bitch would just stop *fucking struggling.*

She shoved the girl backwards, sending her tumbling out of the bathroom and into the hall. The girl scrambled to her feet as Emma stalked towards her. She moved so quickly!

Be patient, she told herself. *Don't let her trick you.*

The girl turned, heading for the stairs.

Emma couldn't allow that to happen.

She gave chase, breaking into a run, pursuing the girl along the hallway. Only then did Emma realize that the trail of blood she had followed to the bathroom had been *planted.* She had been tricked by some teenage bitch.

The idea incensed her.

The girl paused at the top of the stairs. Then she came at Emma, fists swinging chaotically like she had never been in a fight before. There were no tactics. Just the wild, reckless abandon of a junkyard dog, desperate and ferocious. Her blows landed with little real impact, but they were fast, frenzied, and Emma struggled to counter.

She needed a weapon.

The wall was decorated with framed photographs. Emma held up one hand to block the girl's punches, using the other to grab one of the photos. It was a colorful image of a little girl staring out to sea, the sun setting, her back to the camera. She clutched a fishing net in her dainty hand.

Appropriate, thought Emma, as she backhanded the girl with the photo. The corner caught the girl on her cheek, gashing it open. She squealed in pain, then Emma brought the whole thing down on her head, the glass shattering in her hands and raining down around their feet.

The girl staggered, dropping to one knee, resting her hand on the floor for balance.

Emma had her now.

The game was over.

"I'm going to cut you open," said Emma as she took the woozy girl by her hair. "I'm gonna—"

She gasped. The girl was so quick, she hadn't even seen it coming.

Emma looked down at the long shard of glass sticking out of her belly, glass from the photo frame she had broken over the girl's head. She tried to breathe, to ignore the needling agony in her gut. The girl looked up at her.

Was she smiling?

The girl twisted the shard, churning Emma's insides. The room swam, the walls swooning around her. She was losing too much blood.

She stumbled onwards, glass crunching beneath her bare feet.

"You bitch," she said, a familiar coppery tang in her throat. She leaned against the wall, clutching her other hand to her stomach, unable to stem the flow of the blood that surged between her splayed digits.

She was dying, and she knew it.

The girl stood back, watching her, waiting for her to make the next move.

The little bitch was *still fucking smiling*.

Emma took a teetering step forwards. Pain rocketed through her foot from tiny fragments of glass.

"I'm going to kill you," she said, then coughed up a lungful of thick red fluid. There were two of the girl now, identical twins coated in filthy brown bath sludge. Emma staggered towards them, trying to focus. With one final effort, she pounced at one of the figures. It was a fifty-fifty decision.

She chose poorly.

For a fleeting moment, Emma thought she had died. She was floating, weightless. Was she an angel now? Was she ascending to heaven? Had she really lived a good life, enough to allow access through the pearly gates of—

Then her head hit the bottom of the stairs, her body carrying on, snapping her spine at a ninety-degree angle, and Emma thought no more.

Katy wiped the blood from her cheek, wincing as she did so. The cut didn't hurt too badly. Once the adrenaline wore off, it might. For now, though, it was little more than an inconvenience.

Emma stared at her from the lower level, her head bent so far back that the skin around her jugular had torn open. Katy looked at her for a while, at the blood fountaining from her neck, then trudged down the stairs, stepping carefully over Emma's body. Part of her — the part that had once watched *Halloween* with Jill at a sleepover — expected Emma to reach up and grab her one last time.

But she didn't, because the woman was very, very dead.

Katy staggered down the hallway, bumping off the walls. The aerosol flamethrower trick had gone off without a hitch, and although she had expected the fire to kill Varg instantly, she had still managed it. The worst part was pretending she wanted to sleep with him, and the way he had put his hand down his pants.

"Disgusting," she said to herself.

The clock on the wall — this one a red-and-white bouy — read nine-twenty-five. She tried to think. The pick-up was scheduled for twelve. So, presuming Baxter and Corvo had allowed an hour to arrive early, that meant that there would be a two hour drive back. Plus, she assumed they would wait at least an hour for the money to show.

"Okay," said Katy.

She had plenty of time to prepare.

She walked into the downstairs bathroom, turned on the shower, and stepped in fully clothed.

24

Corvo fidgeted in the passenger seat of the van.

"He's not coming," he said.

Baxter checked his watch. Twelve-forty-two. "Give it time. He'll be here soon if he knows what's good for him."

He couldn't understand it. Ketcher should have been and gone by now. Why would he play with his daughter's life like this? It made no sense.

Perspiration trickled down both men's faces as the midday sun reached its apex, glistening off the windows of the gas station across the road.

"I'm hungry," said Corvo.

"You should have eaten before we left," said Baxter. "Didn't you have breakfast?"

Corvo shrugged. "Forgot."

Jesus, thought Baxter. *He's like a child.*

Corvo gazed at the gas station through the windshield. "Might get a sandwich."

"Stay put. Ketcher could arrive any second."

"I won't be long."

Baxter exhaled. Why couldn't he have brought Emma?

Because you can't trust Corvo to keep Varg in check.

"What are you gonna do?" he snapped. "Stroll into the station and show everyone your face?"

"I'll put on the ski mask." He turned to Baxter, smiling, and held the woolen face covering up.

Baxter shook his head, closing his eyes tightly.

"Let me get this straight. You're gonna walk into a gas station with a fucking *mask* on? Great. I give you five seconds before the fucker behind the counter blows you away with a shotgun."

Corvo tucked the ski mask under the seat. "Guess you're right. Man, I'm real hungry though."

"Stop talking."

Corvo did. For a moment, at least.

"Hot in here, huh?" he said, winding down the window.

"Put it back up," said Baxter. "You want people to see you?"

"No," grumbled Corvo.

He rolled the window up and started drumming an irregular rhythm on his thighs.

Baxter checked his watch again. Twelve-forty-four. Time was dragging. An insect landed on the windshield, then flew away. Corvo cleared his throat, taking an eternity to do so. His stomach rumbled noisily.

"Ha, you hear that?" he said. "Man, I'm—"

"Shut up," snapped Baxter, though he was hungry too. For him, breakfast had been a shot of tequila and a packet of chips. He didn't even like tequila, but thought it might impress Emma.

It hadn't.

He flashed back to the previous night, to Emma washing

her jeans with her ass out. If Corvo hadn't picked that exact moment to get a drink of water, who knows how the evening might have progressed?

"What you thinking about?" said Corvo.

"Huh?"

"You're lookin' at me funny."

"No, I'm not."

Corvo muttered something. He pulled his shirt away from his neck and tried to blow on his own chest.

"This thing not have air con?"

"No," said Baxter. Then, quietly, he added, *"Wish it had a fucking ejector seat."*

They sat in merciful, blessed silence. A couple of cars rolled by, none of them stopping. A semi pulled into the station, the driver hopping out of the cab and strolling leisurely into the building. He emerged a few minutes later carrying a Coke. Baxter glared at the ice cold bottle. He imagined rubbing it across his forehead, the condensation trickling down his face. He was so thirsty. It hadn't occurred to him to bring any water. He had assumed Ketcher would turn up on time.

A fair assumption, he reasoned.

"Is it safe to drink your own piss?" said Corvo suddenly.

Baxter glared at him. "What?"

"Doesn't matter," said Corvo. He waited a minute, then said, "So, you and Emma, huh?"

Baxter gripped the steering wheel. "What about us?"

"You know. Last night. You guys were…"

He didn't finish the sentence. Baxter grinned.

"She's good lookin', right?"

"Sure is," said Corvo.

Baxter ran a hand through his sweat-soaked hair.

"I fucked her," he said, and smiled.

"Oh yeah?"

"Yeah." He turned to Corvo. "Fucked her right up the ass. She was *crying* out for more."

"Huh," said Corvo. He didn't sound impressed, and it angered Baxter.

"I made her come *five times,*" he said, hoping for a bigger reaction.

Corvo looked thoughtful. "She your girlfriend?"

Baxter shrugged. "You could say that, yeah."

Corvo said nothing.

A car drove by. It slowed, pulling into the station, and Baxter sat up straight, forgetting about the conversation.

Bingo.

"That's him," he said.

Corvo peered through the window. "You think he drives a Honda Civic?"

"He's smart. Trying to blend in." Baxter smiled appreciatively. This truly was a worthy adversary. "If he turned up in a Ferrari, it would draw attention."

"Oh. So what now?"

"Now... we wait."

A man in denim overalls and nothing else exited the station. He headed towards the car.

"Is he getting gas?" asked Corvo.

"All part of the ruse. He's casing the joint."

"What if he sees us?"

"Doesn't matter. We'll ditch the van soon, drive it into the sea with the girl's body in the back." He chuckled.

The attendant began to fill the Honda.

"I'm not sure it's him," said Corvo.

"Oh, it's him, alright. He's toying with us, making us wait." He scratched at his chin. "Well, Ketcher, this is one dick-measuring contest you ain't gonna win."

The attendant removed the nozzle from the car and bent down to look in the window. A woman leaned out, smiled, and handed him a bill. The attendant tucked it into his pocket and headed inside, wiping sweat from his brow with the back of one grease-stained hand. The Honda pulled out onto the main road, driving into the horizon until it vanished from sight.

"That wasn't him," said Corvo.

Baxter's knuckles whitened. "I know," he muttered.

"That was a woman."

"I realize that," he said through gritted teeth.

Corvo turned to him, a quizzical look on his broad, shiny face. "I thought you said that was—"

"I know!" screamed Baxter. He punched Corvo on the arm, two times, three times, not hard, but enough to work off some of his frustration. "I know! I fucking know it's not him, Jesus fucking Christ, I know!"

He opened the door and jumped out of the van, kicking up dust as he landed. It wasn't any cooler outside. There was no wind, no breeze. Just a cloying humidity. He paced around the van, checking his watch.

Twelve-forty-eight.

They had been here for over two hours, waiting like a pair of jackasses for a delivery that wasn't coming. Ketcher had tricked him. What if the cops showed up? He glanced neurotically across the landscape, searching for the flash of police lights, the whir of a helicopter, or the glint of light reflecting off a sniper rifle's sights.

It was a set up. He realized it now. Kevin Ketcher had refused to pay, and now the FBI would descend. They had to get back to the lodge.

What if they're already there?

They couldn't be, not yet. Unless they had traced the

call. And why not? The girl had used her own phone. God! He was so stupid.

Baxter hurried to the open door, throwing himself into the driver's seat.

"What's going on?" said Corvo, but Baxter had already turned the keys, the engine rumbling into life. The wheels skidded on the gravel, and then the van was thundering down the road, the gas station vanishing in the heat haze of the unforgiving midday sun.

Katy Ketcher sat on the porch and waited.

At sixteen, she had never considered what it would be like to grow old. She lived her life day-to-day, never thinking further ahead than the weekend, or — at a push — summer.

But now, rocking gently on an old wooden chair with a hunting rifle on her lap, she wondered if this was what growing up felt like. It wasn't so bad, she supposed, sitting in the heat and listening to the caw of the gulls, the break of the waves against the sand.

It was a beautiful day.

Her clothes had dried in the sun, though the repugnant odor of death lingered. An unopened can of beer perched on the wooden table by her side, and she cracked it open with a satisfying fizz. She drank, then spat the liquid out.

"That's gross," she said.

That's what getting old is all about. Putting aside childish thoughts and notions, and learning to adapt. To beer. To death.

To murder.

She took a smaller sip, determined to keep it down, wondering how her father managed to drink this stuff with supper every night. She remained there a while, one hand resting on the rifle, bizarrely at peace with herself. Two phones lay on the table, and she put the drink down and picked one up. Originally, it had been locked by fingerprint recognition, much like her own, but that had been an easy obstacle to overcome. She had simply pressed Emma's lifeless finger against the device to open it, then adjusted the settings to remove the lock. She supposed a dead person didn't really care if you used their phone or not. What happened after *that* was a little weird, but Katy decided not to think about it right now. The deed was done. All she had to do now was send the photo to Baxter.

She couldn't finish the beer. It was already making her head feel funny. She got up, sad to leave the serene motion of the rocking chair behind, and placed the can on the porch railing. Then she picked up the rifle and walked steadily to the other end of the porch. She had retrieved the pistol from the murky bathwater, but the barrel was clogged up and wouldn't fire. Instead, she had used it to batter a thin padlock from a locked door on the ground floor. Behind that door she had found a storage cupboard stocked with fishing supplies. Rods, nets, hooks, a toolbox, a small axe... and the hunting rifle.

She wished she had found a weapon that was lighter, easier to carry... but she would make do. Squinting into the sun, Katy raised the weapon to her shoulder, lined up her shot, and fired. The bullet zipped harmlessly past the can. She tried again, aiming lower, and this time the bullet thudded into the wooden railing.

She took a deep breath, steadied herself.

Everything is ready. You got this.

Be the—

She squeezed the trigger and the can pinged from the

railing, spraying white foam in every direction. It landed satisfyingly in the sand.

"Be the pug," she smiled.

She opened Emma's phone again and hit Send on the message.

Now, all she could do was wait.

25

———

IT WAS AFTER THREE WHEN THE FISHING LODGE SHIMMERED into view through the late afternoon heat-haze. Baxter drove slowly, one hand on the wheel, the other clutching his phone, re-reading Emma's message for the twentieth time.

Katy's dad called. Cash wasn't ready, had no way to contact us. Will bring it tomorrow. Apologized. Begged us not to hurt her. No problem. When you get back, keep Corvo in the van. I'll be waiting upstairs. You'll know where to find me. X

When he first read it, he immediately knew something was off.

Katy?

Since when had they referred to her by name? Emma knew the codeword was "the package." Hell, she had come up with it herself, and it wasn't like Emma to break protocol. The thought would have played on his mind all the way home, were it not for the attached photo.

It was Emma. Or, more specifically, Emma's bare breasts. He glanced at the image again, the odd use of language in Emma's message the farthest thing from his thoughts. His anger at the aborted pick-up faded, replaced by an excited throbbing in his trousers that clouded his mind with delicious fantasies.

She wanted him. He didn't even have the money yet, and she *wanted* him.

Keep Corvo in the van.

How the hell was he supposed to do that? Corvo was an idiot, but he couldn't be expected to sit in the van for another hour or two in the height of summer.

You'll think of something.

He wondered why she had changed her mind. It had to be the thought of all that money. Five million each. It was almost too much. Baxter was a man of simple pleasures. He didn't need a mansion, or an expensive car, or a private island... he just wanted to never work again, and to have a good woman to fuck. Anything more than that was pure greed. Kevin Ketcher was a multi-millionaire. According to a Google search, he owned properties in New York, LA, and San Francisco, along with summer residences in at least three unnamed states. Then there were his European getaways, his collection of vintage cars... and his daughter. That spoiled brat would never have to work a day in her life, and why? Because her daddy had made a few movies? It wasn't fair. The pair of them made him sick. Well, he would take from them the one thing money couldn't buy... the little bitch's *life*.

He was getting angry again, so he snuck a look at Emma's tits on his phone.

God, they were perfect. And soon they would be his.

"Whatcha looking at?" said Corvo.

Baxter shoved the phone between his legs. "Nothing." Then, remembering he needed an excuse, added, "Em says get more firewood. You need to go along the beach and collect some."

"A fire? Why? I was so hot, I had to sleep naked last night."

"I don't need to fucking know that. Maybe she wants to burn the bodies? It doesn't matter. Do as she says."

"But there's no wood around here."

"Look for driftwood, asshole. And don't come back until you've found enough to light up the fucking sky, you hear me?"

"Yeah, sure," muttered Corvo.

The van rounded the final bend. It was a straight line all the way back now. Baxter thought he saw movement in one of the upstairs windows.

Emma. Waiting for him.

He wondered what she'd done with Varg.

Had she disposed of him? It wouldn't surprise him. Varg had done nothing to help. If it wasn't for Corvo's big mouth, the creep would be at home fucking a blow-up doll right now, or shooting up a high school. He was better off dead. They would be doing the world a favor.

He parked by the side of the lodge and left the van, stretching his legs, eager to get upstairs and find Emma. He hoped she hadn't changed her mind.

Corvo shoved his hands in his pockets. "Guess I'll go look for that wood."

I got plenty in my pants, thought Baxter.

"You do that," he said. "Get enough to, I dunno, fill the back of the van or something."

"Aw man, that's crazy."

"Hey, it's Emma. You know what she's like."

But not like me. I'm about to find out the noise she makes when she comes.

Corvo nodded, sulking away towards the beach like a surly teenager grudgingly doing what his father told him.

That makes you *the father.*

Baxter smiled.

"Then I'd better go upstairs and fuck mommy," he whispered.

Feeling good, he walked to the porch and let himself in. The lodge was quiet. He stood a moment, listening for Emma, or for Varg.

Silence.

She had killed him. She *had* to have killed him. It would explain both the silence, and also her horniness. He remembered how she acted after killing the old man. She was blood-crazy.

Baxter went back to the front door and peered out. Corvo was struggling through the sand, stooping occasionally to pick up a twig. He'd be gone for hours at this rate.

"Idiot," chuckled Baxter as he quietly closed the door and headed for the bathroom. He passed the cellar. Out of instinct, he reached for the handle and tried it.

The door was unlocked.

"Fucking amateurs," he sighed. The hinges wailed theatrically as he pushed the door open and gazed into the darkness, waiting for his eyes to adjust. The stench of decay hit him. It was overpowering. The girl's friend must be rotting. Shit, there wasn't much he could do about that. He took a step into the cellar.

His phone vibrated.

Another message from Emma.

You coming up? I'm lonely. X

His stomach lurched in excitement.

"Ah, fuck it," he grinned. He closed the cellar door, locked it, and shoved the key in his pocket. Hurrying to the bathroom, he quickly pissed and checked his reflection in the mirror, annoyed at the dark sweat-stains on his shirt. He peeled the wet garment from his body and dumped it in the basin, his anticipation nearing fever pitch.

She was up there, waiting for him.

He decided to leave the shirt to soak and head up topless. Might as well give her a treat. Sure, he was no Corvo in the muscles department, but nor was he a skinny freak like Varg. He reached the foot of the stairs, where a single sneaker waited for him.

It belonged to Emma.

There was another sneaker a few steps up, lying on its side, the laces untied. Baxter smiled. Three steps up from the sneaker was Emma's discarded vest. He picked it up, then dropped it and continued his ascent, paying scant attention to the bloodstains on the wall.

Must be Varg's, he figured, stepping over Emma's abandoned jeans and licking his parched lips. He wondered what Emma had done with his body? Probably down in the cellar with the little bitch. The idea pleased him. The girl was more trouble than she was worth. What should have been a simple transaction was turning into a fiasco.

Baxter reached the top of the stairs. Emma's bra lay to his left, outside the door to the room where Emma slept.

"Oh, I'm coming baby," he whispered. "I'm coming to show you a *real* good time."

He made his way along the hallway, trying to stay cool, and stopped by the door. The knowledge that Emma waited behind it drove him crazy. He rapped his knuckles against the wood.

No answer.

That little tease! Giving him the silent treatment. Well, he'd make her talk. Hell, he'd make her squeal.

He opened the door.

The ragged curtains were drawn, but he could make out the bed, the duvet bundled up around her.

"Hey," he said slyly. "Daddy's home."

He winced. That was *not* a good line.

Maybe just shut up for now?

Good idea.

The door closed behind him, but Emma did not stir. She was toying with him. He kicked off his shoes, then dropped his pants. He didn't need to remove his underwear, because he wasn't wearing any.

As he lifted the duvet and slid under the covers, he noticed the girl's schoolbag on the floor by the bed, a box of bullets balanced on top. What had Emma been up to? Target practise, with Varg as the target?

Varget practise, he thought absurdly.

He snuggled alongside Emma, his hands stroking the softness of her skin. She was icy cold.

"Hey baby," he said. "Want me to warm you up?"

He ran his hands up her soft flesh, kneading it between his fingers, pressing his chest against her back. He kissed her neck, pulling her towards him, his calloused hands finding her breasts, kneading them.

She didn't react.

His erection was strong, and he pressed it against her ass. She still had her panties on.

"Let's get these off, shall we?" he cooed, sliding one hand down from her breast, across her smooth, flat stomach towards her—

What the fuck?

His fingers probed unfamiliar territory, sliding into a tight, wet hole.

"Hey," he said, but something wasn't right. Something wasn't right *at all*. Her pussy was too high. Fuck, it was on her *stomach,* just below her bellybutton. He withdrew his hand.

Emma was too quiet.

Baxter put his hand to his mouth and licked the juices from his fingers. His stomach flipped.

It was blood.

"Jesus," he said, recoiling. He scrambled out of bed and drew the covers back.

The light came on. He had a second to register the pale, blood-soaked body of Emma before a voice spoke.

"Don't move," it said.

Baxter knew exactly who it was.

He stood with his back to her, naked and disgusting, the tips of his fingers red with blood.

Adrenaline surged through Katy's veins.

He spun to face her, freezing when he realized he was literally staring down the barrel of a gun.

"Surprised?" she asked, adjusting the hunting rifle to hide his penis from her sight. He was uncomfortably close to her, and she took a couple of steps back.

"Listen," he said, holding up his hand in a calming gesture. "Don't do anything stupid."

"Too late. You don't want to piss off a teenage girl. I've already killed Emma and Varg, and I feel like being *pretty* stupid."

He inched forwards, and she raised the gun towards his face.

"Did you not hear me?" she said. "I *killed* them. You think I won't kill you too?"

"You can't have done. You're just a girl. You're just a *kid.*"

He turned away from her, gazing at Emma's body lying prone on the bed, a small wound on her stomach, the sheets crimson. Her neck was a grisly purple bruise, the skin torn and frayed. Baxter nodded slowly and faced her again. "So what now?"

"Now, I kill you. And when Corvo comes back, I kill him too."

Baxter broke into a lopsided grin. "Guess we underestimated you."

"Looks like it."

He sighed and glanced at Emma again. "I loved her, you know."

Katy kept her eyes trained on Baxter. She saw his fingers twitch.

"Don't move," she said.

He laughed at her. "I'm not afraid of you, little girl. You wouldn't—"

The gun went off, ear-splittingly loud in the confines of the bedroom. Emma's body shook as the bullet rippled into her lifeless torso. Katy and Baxter locked eyes.

"That was a warning," she hissed. She lowered the gun towards his crotch. "Next time I won't miss."

"What do you want?" he said. "Huh? What the *fuck* do you want?"

"I want to know why. I want to know if it was worth it. You killed my friend. Why?"

He spat on the floor. "I never touched her."

"You're scum, you know that? You can't even take responsibility. I'm a kid, and my dad and my teachers tell me I have to take responsibility. That's what *adults* do. We can't say *it's not fair*, we can't blame others. We make our own decisions and face up to our actions. It's what growing up is all about, so don't tell me you weren't involved."

"Oh, just fucking shoot me," said Baxter. "I'm not gonna be lectured by a fucking *kid*. You're not old enough to be telling me what to do."

"But I'm old enough to be kidnapped, right? I'm old enough to be beaten, and gagged, and locked in a cellar? I'm old enough to watch my friend get murdered?"

He shook his head. "You tried to escape," he said in a petulant whine.

"Wouldn't you?"

"No one would kidnap me. I'm not worth anything."

"At last we agree on something."

He laughed at that. "You know, you're all right, kid. I did underestimate you. Big time. Guess the joke's on me." He looked down at his jeans. "Mind if I put these on? Or you gonna kill me with my big dick flopping about?"

"Go ahead." She glanced at it. She'd never seen one before in real life. "Doesn't look that big."

He half-smiled and bent to pick up his pants, staring at her. She refused to give in to his mind games, and held the eye contact. It was her one mistake, but it was a big one. She didn't see his hand slide into his pants pocket.

He knew what he was doing. He was quick.

By the time he pulled the switchblade out, he had already pressed the button. The blade shot out as he threw the knife in an upward trajectory. It spun through the air lightning fast. The point speared Katy's thigh. She screamed and squeezed the trigger, firing into the window, the glass shattering, and then Baxter was hurtling towards her. She swung the rifle, catching him on the side of the head with the stock, but he was already in the air. His body collided with hers, and together they crashed into the wall and hit the ground.

Baxter's weight pinned her down, and demented red

panic clouded her mind. The gun was trapped between their writhing bodies, pointing uselessly off to the side. He punched her in the face, the pain not enough to take her mind off the knife sticking out of her leg.

The knife.

Baxter raised his fist again, and she reached down, finding the knife, jerking it free from her thigh. He noticed the movement, watching as she thrust the switchblade towards his face. He raised his hand in time for the knife to catch him in the palm, exploding through the back of his hand with a jet of blood.

Thinking fast, Katy dragged the knife free, trying desperately to stab him again. This time he blocked her with his arm, the switchblade penetrating it below the elbow. Blood gushed from the wounds, but she kept a firm grip on the handle. Before she knew what was happening, Baxter had thrown himself backwards, taking the rifle with him. He raised it up, aiming for her, but his right arm was badly damaged and he struggled to pull the trigger. It bought her enough time to leap behind the bed as Baxter fired wildly off the mark.

"You cunt!" he shouted. "You fucking cunt!"

With the gun shaking in his hands, he kicked her schoolbag to the side, the box of bullets bursting open, the contents rattling across the floor. Katy shuffled her way under the bed, watching his feet as he moved. Ignoring the pain in her leg, she gripped the knife in her small hand and stabbed it into his ankle. The man screamed, taking a stumbling step backwards and falling.

Katy crawled out from under the bed. She saw Baxter struggling with the rifle, and considered attacking with the switchblade again, but then she remembered something Varg had said.

Someone comes at you with a weapon, you find a bigger one.

The knife was too small. It was useless. She fled the room, limping on her damaged leg. Behind her, Baxter scrambled to his feet.

Katy reached into her shirt pocket and pulled out a handful of fishing hooks she had found in the storage room. She let them fall from her hands and kept running as best as her injured leg would allow. Baxter's feet pounded the floorboards. Seconds later she heard him roar in agony. She turned to see him hopping on one foot, the metal hooks digging into the hard flesh of his sole.

Part of her wanted nothing more than to stay and watch him pluck the sharpened talons from his feet, but he still held the rifle. She needed to find a better weapon. She remembered the axe in the storage cupboard downstairs. If she could just get to it...

She ran. She was almost at the stairs when she heard the click of the trigger. Instinctively, she fell to the ground, covering her head.

But there were no more gunshots. The rifle was out of ammo.

Thank god!

As she tried to get to her feet, something hard and heavy smacked into her spine. She crumpled as the rifle stock made contact. Rolling onto her back, she saw Baxter hobbling above her. He raised the rifle above his head, ready to bring it down on her face. She had no more than a second until he crushed her skull. Her hand shot up reflexively. There was a flash of silver as brief and fleeting as a heartbreak, before the switchblade sliced through Baxter's scrotum like butter.

"Jesus, fuck," he screamed, his voice a feverish, anguished howl. The rifle clunked to the floor. He doubled over, hands

grasping at his groin, a river of blood cascading down his legs. Katy crawled away, scrabbling towards the stairs as he stumbled after her. He stopped, bumping into the wall, staying there a moment. A constant, whining moan whistled from his lips like a punctured tire. She watched in disbelief as he staggered back to the rifle, picking it up with tremendous difficulty. He propped himself up with it, staring at her with cold, furious eyes, then stomped towards the bedroom.

Katy tried to stand, the searing pain in her thigh impeding her attempts. Crawling to the stairs, she used the handrail to haul herself up. She looked towards the bedroom expectantly, her gaze following the thick trail of dark black blood left by Baxter.

Surely he couldn't survive much longer.

You could have run.

Even at a time like this, the voice in her head wanted to argue. She ignored it, pressing a hand to her thigh. It burned. One of her white school socks was drenched in blood. She could feel it sloshing around in her boot.

Baxter appeared in the hallway, teetering into the wall, still covering his torn testicles. He stared at her, then vomited a mixture of puke and blood down his bare chest.

"Just die," said Katy.

He shook his head, wobbling back and forth like a drunken sailer, and raised the gun, aiming with one hand.

It's empty, she was about to say, until she remembered the bullets scattered across the bedroom floor. That must have been why he went back.

To reload.

The staircase loomed to her left. Katy recalled the way Emma had fallen down it, snapping her neck in the process.

Baxter steadied his aim.

She had no choice.

Katy threw herself down the stairs as he pulled the trigger. The bullet grazed her upper arm, ripping through her shirt and shearing off a layer of skin. She screamed as she tumbled gracelessly down the flight of stairs, curling into a protective ball. It didn't help. She smacked her head and jarred her bones on each step before landing in a heap. Dazed, she peered up the stairs as Baxter followed. He took aim once more. The wooden floorboard in front of her face erupted in splinters and smoke as he fired again.

Go, go!

Where?

Then she had an idea. It hadn't worked before, but surely this time...

With a burst of lunatic strength borne of self-preservation, Katy willed her legs to work, to carry her towards the cellar, towards the missing third step. After disposing of Emma, Katy had added her own little twist — twenty nails hammered at an angle into the steps above and below it. If someone was to slip through that gap now, their back and chest would be torn to shreds. She had spent most of the afternoon doing it... and who better to fall into her trap than Baxter?

The cellar door was close. She could make it. She had to.

Searing pain flared up her leg, blood pumping from the wound. Katy dropped to one knee, clasping a hand over her thigh. The room swam. She tried to stand but couldn't, collapsing woozily onto her stomach, gasping for breath.

She heard the *thump, thump* of the rifle on the stairs as Baxter falteringly made his way down.

Hurry!

She looked back at the trail of blood she had left across the floor.

Too much blood.

She couldn't make it. It was over. How could she reach the door when she couldn't even stand? She had failed. Even with time to plan, to think things through, she had messed everything up.

"I'm sorry, Jill," she whimpered. Something clattered down the stairs behind her. The rifle. She looked back to see Baxter swaying precariously halfway down. He gripped the railing with one hand, the other still clutching feverishly at his testicles, and took a groggy step down.

Move!

She tried to stand again, but it was hopeless. Her leg was numb. The door was only feet away, but it may as well have been miles. She was going to die, killed by a man with his balls hanging out. What a way to go.

Don't give up! Be the pug!

What did that even mean? Such a stupid phrase. She closed her eyes and thought of Balloon licking her nose, barking at a toy that had fallen from the sofa, crawling under the table to retrieve a morsel of food, dragging himself forwards by his tiny paws...

Exactly. If he could do it, so can you!

Katy stretched her arm out, digging her nails into a gap between the floorboards. She pulled herself forwards, her body scraping along the floor.

That's it!

Baxter had to be close now, but she didn't look round. She held both trembling arms out and hooked her nails into the floor, using her fingers to drag herself. The nail on her index finger snapped off, but she barely noticed. She was making progress.

Baxter's body thudded behind her. He had reached the ground floor. Katy moved forwards, kicking against the floor with her good leg, the cellar door looming before her. She reached out, stretching, *stretching,* her hand grasping the handle, a grim smile breaking across her face. She yanked the handle down, and—

It was locked.

She tried again, putting her weight into it, hanging from the metal handle...

But the door wouldn't budge.

How? She had deliberately left it unlocked in case of emergency, in case everything had gone wrong and she had to escape to the cellar.

Baxter must have done it. When he arrived back at the lodge, he must have locked it.

"No," she said, slumping against the door. *"No."*

Tears came. She knew it was over. She had been a fool to think she could pull this off herself, one girl against four adults. The whole venture was doomed from the start. It took a lot to kill someone. Not mentally. That part was easy. These people had killed her friend, and so she had killed them.

It was quite simple, really.

What she hadn't counted on was how difficult it was to actually make someone die. It took a long time. The human body was resilient. The amount of punishment it could withstand was shocking.

Baxter shuffled towards her. His face was as pale as a long-dead moon, his movements labored and arthritic. He used the rifle as a cane, leaning heavily on it. Looking down at her with hazy, bloodshot eyes, he raised the gun, holding it at waist height, the barrel swaying relentlessly left-to-right, left-to-right.

"I got you now," he slurred. "And tomorrow, your daddy'll bring the money." He smiled a hellish, broken smile. "Looks like I won, bitch."

Wait, he still thinks—

Katy couldn't help it.

She started to laugh.

She laughed, and laughed, and laughed, the dreadful tears of pain giving way to floods of hilarity.

"What's so funny?" said Baxter. It sounded like, "Whas-ssso funneh?"

Katy wiped away the tears and looked back at him through clouded eyes.

"I never even called him, you *dork,*" she said. "He doesn't even know I'm gone. He's on location." She snorted out a belly laugh and shook her head. "I'm home alone all week."

Baxter breathed a deep, rattling sigh. It seemed to take forever for him to understand what she had said. Katy didn't mind. The look on his face was priceless. It made everything worthwhile.

"Looks like we both lose," she said, and laughed again.

"I can still call him," he said. "I can—"

"I called the cops."

He looked at her for a long time. "No. I don't think you did."

She shrugged and leaned her head back against the locked door.

"Guess you'll find out," she smiled.

He raised the gun, nearly losing his balance. His face — his entire *body* — was pure white, apart from the deep streaks of crimson that poured from his arm, his hand, his mutilated balls.

The barrel swung back and forth like a pendulum. He closed one of his eyes, and she thought for one glorious second that he was going to drop dead.

But it was not to be.

"*Fuck... you,*" he said, and pulled the trigger.

The shot went wide.

There was an eardrum-shattering sound of metal striking metal as the bullet hit the door handle and ricocheted into the wall, and then Katy was falling backwards, the door opening behind her, the lock and handle clanging to the floor.

"*Fuck!*" she heard Baxter shout as she tumbled head-over-heels into the cellar, bouncing over the missing step with its sharp, waiting nails, hitting most of the rest of the stairs on the way down.

She struck the packed dirt of the cellar floor with a bone-rattling jolt.

Somehow, she found herself laughing again.

"You missed!" she cried, tears rolling down her face, the salty liquid stinging the gaping wound in her cheek. Her entire body throbbed. She lay on her back, unable to move. All she could do now was wait for Baxter to follow her.

His silhouette filled the door frame, hunched and misshapen like a zombie from that dumb show her dad watched.

The Walking Dead.

Yeah, that one. She had nicknamed him The Walking Dad after it, which had annoyed him tremendously.

"You're dead, bitch," said Baxter.

The rifle fell from his hand, and he gripped the bannister, balancing on the top step.

"Come and get me, then," said Katy, surprised she was still able to speak. Nothing else seemed to be working.

"I'm going to rip your fucking throat out."

"You'll have to catch me first," she said.

Yeah, that'll be difficult.

He placed one foot on the second step down, and then the other.

"I'm gonna slice your tits off."

"I'm right here, you pussy. *Come and get me!*"

One more step. Just one more step.

He removed his hand from his crotch, and something plopped out onto the step between his feet. "My balls," he cried. "You took my fucking *balls.*"

He bent slowly, stooping to pick up the errant testicle, and then he saw it.

The missing step.

He looked at Katy. It was his turn to laugh, though it sounded more like the wailing of the damned.

"Nice try," he said, forcing his leg forward, striding clumsily over the void. His other foot followed, and then he was clear. "You almost got me."

Shit.

So that was it then. Her last chance to survive, thwarted by a testicle.

That would make a great title for your autobiography, she thought. *Katy Ketcher: Thwarted By A Testicle.*

She was losing it. She supposed death did funny things to your brain.

Baxter reached the foot of the stairs, standing before her.

"I'm going to beat your fucking brains in," he said, glancing around the cellar. He spotted Varg, the rogue step lying beside his battered and burned head. Baxter wrenched it from Varg's skull and staggered towards her.

Katy closed her eyes.

Sixteen years old.

It wasn't a long time to be alive.

Sixteen years.

That's eight years older than Balloon had been when her father had taken him to the vet, never to return.

She thought of that day, of how upset she had been, of how everything else had paled into insignificance.

She thought of Balloon's round eyes, so sad and vulnerable.

And she thought of her father coming home, of his tear-streaked face, and of how he hadn't said a word to her, just shaken his head and held her as she wept.

"I love you, Balloon," she whispered.

Baxter squinted at her, a string of blood-flecked saliva dangling from his lips. "You're fucking crazy," he said, his shredded scrotum hanging like net curtains.

"You can't always be the pug," she said. "But you can try."

He looked at her as if she had gone mad.

"The only thing I hate more than rich little bitches like you," he said, the words coming in ponderous gasps, "are fucking *pugs.*"

Katy smiled sadly. "And pugs hate *you,*" she said.

"Fuck you," said Baxter, and he raised the plank of wood above his head.

A booming, cacophonous explosion ripped through the cellar.

Baxter's body stiffened. He tried to turn, stumbling, and then fell to his knees. Another gunshot resonated throughout the cramped space, and this time Baxter's face disappeared in a welter of blood and bone. The plank clattered to the floor, followed by a single testicle. It rolled across the floor and nudged Katy's foot. With her last reserve of strength, she stamped down on it with a wet squelch.

Someone stood in the doorway, clutching the hunting rifle. A thin plume of smoke wafted from the barrel.

"Are you okay?" said Corvo. "I heard gunshots. I ran as fast as I could."

Katy looked up at him. Her eyes flickered shut, and she forced them open.

"You saved my life," she said.

Corvo cast the rifle aside and started down the stairs. "I promised I wouldn't let them hurt you. I—"

He never noticed the missing step.

27

It was one of those postcard moments.

The setting sun, its orange brilliance flaring across the ocean, the black silhouette of the abandoned fishing lodge a painterly addition to the landscape. All was still for miles around, except for the furtive movements of wildlife and the ice-age drift of the clouds.

A curious otter darted from behind the white van, scampering along the driveway and up towards the lodge. It sniffed and listened, suddenly on high alert. The front door groaned open, and the otter fled back to where it had come from.

Katy Ketcher leaned against the doorway. The fresh air hit her like a nuclear bomb. She breathed it in until her lungs were full, never wanting to let it out. Her schoolbag hung from one shoulder. She didn't know how long it had taken her to climb the steps from the cellar, but it was nothing compared to the staircase to the bedroom. After that, Mount Everest would be a piece of cake. On the way down, she had sat on the steps, bouncing her ass down one at a time. It was the only part of her that didn't hurt.

So Jill was right, huh, fat ass?

She supposed so. Jill was *always* right.

She stepped out onto the porch with the sun in her eyes, blinding in the most beautiful way. Placing her bag on the wobbly wooden table, she settled her aching body into the rocking chair. From her bag, she took a beer, the last one from the fridge. It took her a further ten minutes to muster the strength to open it, and when she sipped it, she still hated the taste.

"Better than nothing," she said to the wind.

She could still hear Corvo's anguished screams, but they were quieter now, and blended with the squawks of the hungry gulls. If he didn't shut up soon, she'd have to retrieve the axe from the storage cupboard and put him out of his misery.

He can wait. Take it easy. You deserve it.

The sea welcomed the sun into its bosom, and soon it was dark, the stars twinkling like midnight jewelry. She took another drink and actually managed to swallow the amber liquid. In time, she would get used to it, she supposed. She had gotten used to a lot over the last few days.

Something howled in the distance, the sound carrying across the dunes, and she shivered. It was getting cold.

No problem. She emptied the contents of her bag onto the table. Two phones — one hers, one Emma's — a back-up battery pack, some gum, her notebooks, but most importantly, a blanket she had taken from the easy chair in the bedroom. With infinitesimal care, she wrapped it around her shoulders, then plugged the back-up battery into the phone and waited for it to charge.

She took another sip of beer.

Yeah, she could see herself living in a place like this.

One day.

For now, she had the rest of her life to live.

AFTERWORD

Way back in 2019, I needed a break from writing *Dead Girl Blues*, which was a very difficult book in terms of both its complicated mystery structure and the overall heaviness of its subject matter. I needed to write something a little... lighter. And so my mind wandered — as it often does — to *Home Alone*, and what a slightly more realistic version of that perennial holiday classic would be like.

Thus, *The Perfect Victim* was born. I wrote the first half, popped it in a drawer, and resumed work on *Dead Girl Blues*. I was particularly pleased with a fun scene where Katy attempts to manipulate Corvo by discussing the slogan on his shirt.

RESTORE THE SNYDERVERSE, it originally said, referring to the mythical 'Snyder Cut' of Zac Snyder's *Justice League,* which we all knew would never, *ever* be released.

Cut to a year later, and we're in the middle of a pandemic. I was furloughed from my day job. I'd finished my fourth book Maggie's Grave, I'd written the first draft of a western horror with Steve Stred... so what now? I dug out The Perfect Victim and went to work, finishing the story just in time for Zack Snyder to announce the release of his director's cut of *Justice League*.

Damn you, Snyder! You've instantly dated my book before it's even been published! Well, you snooze, you lose, I guess.

Never mind. The whole *Star Wars* fanboy fiasco worked just as well, I think.

As ever, I hope you enjoyed my story. Though it was planned as being a bit lighter, things definitely got darker in the second half. I dearly love a major tonal shift in a story, something I believe comes from growing up watching movies from Hong Kong and South Korea, where slapstick comedy can give way to brutal violence in the blink of an eye. I often see people lament the 'tonal inconsistencies' of these films, but I believe that criticism is rooted in a fundamentally western view of storytelling, where a specific tone must seemingly be maintained at all times.

Look at Bong Joon-Ho's South Korean *Memories of Murder,* with its running gag of people falling down a hill intercut with dark scenes of grotesque violence, or Hong Kong director Clarence Fok Yiu-Leung's *Naked Killer,* a sizzling erotic thriller with a comic scene where a detective accidentally eats a severed penis. Or what about Boaz Davidson's Israeli sex comedy *Lemon Popsicle,* with its unforgettably downbeat ending?

If those films are all 'tonally inconsistent,' then I am 100% here for it.

~

As always, thanks to my lovely wife Heather for her support and encouragement.

Cheers to Boris, whose antics inspired the character of Balloon.

Big thanks to Gemma Amor for her sterling cover art. She's a superbly talented author too, check out her books!

Thanks to my beta readers Steve Stred, Andy Marr, Heather Hood, Emily Cardwell, John Bender, and Johann Trotter.

And thanks once more to you, dear reader. Wherever you are, and whatever you do, never forget — *be the pug.*

As usual, I'll leave you with my writing playlist, though for once I don't suggest listening along as you read. This book was written to some early 90s Swedish death metal, which doesn't particularly go with the story. Or maybe it does, who knows?

Dismember — *Like An Ever Flowing Stream*
Dismember — *Indecent and Obscene*
Entombed — *Left Hand Path*
Entombed — *Clandestine*
Grave — *Into The Grave*
Grave — *You'll Never See*

ALSO BY DAVID SODERGREN

The Forgotten Island
Night Shoot
Dead Girl Blues
Maggie's Grave
The Navajo Nightmare (with Steve Stred)

ABOUT THE AUTHOR

David Sodergren lives in Scotland with his wife Heather and his best friend, Boris the Pug. Growing up, he was the kind of kid who collected rubber skeletons and lived for horror movies.
Not much has changed since then.
He has published six horror novels — The Forgotten Island, Night Shoot, Dead Girl Blues, Maggie's Grave, and The Navajo Nightmare (with Steve Stred), and The Perfect Victim.

Twitter — @paperbacksnpugs
Instagram — @paperbacksandpugs